SNAKE ISLAND

SNAKE ISLAND

A NOVEL

BEN HOBSON

ARCADE
CRIMEWISE

An Arcade CrimeWise Book

First North American Edition 2020

This is a work of fiction. Names, places, characters, and incidents are either the products of the author's imagination or are used fictitiously.

Arcade Publishing books may be purchased in bulk at special discounts for sales promotion, corporate gifts, fund-raising, or educational purposes. Special editions can also be created to specifications. For details, contact the Special Sales Department, Arcade Publishing, 307 West 36th Street, 11th Floor, New York, NY 10018 or arcade@skyhorsepublishing.com.

Arcade Publishing® and CrimeWise® are registered trademarks of Skyhorse Publishing, Inc.®, a Delaware corporation.

Visit the author's site at hobsonben.wordpress.com.
Visit our website at www.arcadepub.com.

10 9 8 7 6 5 4 3 2 1

Library of Congress Control Number: 2020940060
Library of Congress Cataloging-in-Publication Data is available on file.

Cover design by Luke Causby/Blue Cork, courtesy of Allen & Unwin

ISBN: 978-1-950691-71-5
Ebook ISBN: 978-1-951627-23-2

Printed in the United States of America

For Aunty Rose
If you're reading this, and you don't know
who I'm talking about, you missed out.

SNAKE ISLAND

ONE

~

VERNON MOORE

The weight of a life, summed up in the suffering. Look at the bloody thing. Vernon had noticed the downed bird as he lowered himself into his chair, mug of tea in hand, and sat at a loss. He should get up. Though there wasn't much could be done. One white wing, caked in muck, rose above its body. No seeing the orange beak. None of the elegance normally bestowed upon a pelican remained. It was muddy black and it was dying and that was all. Out on the mudflats of Port Napier. Behind it, Snake Island. The tide would drown it, though not for a while. Like it drowned everything eventually. With the polar ice caps melting it wouldn't be long before all humanity was underwater. The sea was never full, would never stop eating. He'd be in it too, one day.

He'd heard somewhere, no telling where or when with his age, that pelicans were once revered creatures, that people had believed that a mother bird, to avoid her young starving, would strike at her own breast and feed them from her wounds. That she'd give her blood, her life, that they might continue on. Vernon chortled into his tea, splashing some onto his trouser leg. He brushed at it, angered. Bloody superstitious nonsense. Probably something he'd overheard that history teacher in the staffroom yammering on about. Old bloke. Long dead by now, surely. What had his name been? Couldn't bloody ever shut up. He'd be talking to the worms in his coffin now he was dead. About pelicans and bloody that bloke who was killed by his enemies with a poker shoved in his arse like he was turned on a spit—the king?—and who knows what else.

He watched the bird as it choked in air but the wing above, the flag, never dropped. He finished his tea and still it waved. He sighed, went inside to the kitchen and found the key to his toolshed. Gumbooted, he strode across his meagre back lawn and unlocked the shed and put the padlock and key on a terracotta pot beside the door. He surveyed the shed. The shotgun on the back shelf and the box of shells nearby. Not sure about that. He handled the axe in the corner and decided.

He climbed down the stone embankment skirting their property and entered the mud. It sucked immediately at his gumboots and he struggled with each step to pull them free without leaving them behind and dunking his socks in the slop. During high tide the water would slosh right up to their back garden, covering where he stood, but now, with the tide out, there was just this muddy expanse. Soldier crabs jutted from their burrows and scooted back inside as he came near. And seaweed, big brown ropes of it, almost everywhere he walked. He had the axe resting over his shoulder.

As he reached the pelican he saw the cause of its suffering. From its proud beak protruded a small bit of plastic, the type used to carry a six-pack. Vernon sat down on his haunches. The eyes of the bird were alarmed but the wing had finally fallen. Perhaps the creature had only desired another with which to share its death. The smell of brine so strong. Vernon attempted a tug on the plastic but it was so embedded he feared pulling up the guts with it.

He was angered at his lack of forethought. No real way of swinging the axe out here. It'd sink into the muddy sand and wouldn't lop the head off at all and simply cause the bird further pain. He didn't want to have to swing the axe twice, hacking at the neck like he was splitting wood. Should've brought the gun.

He moved the pelican's head so the neck was vulnerable. The poor bird couldn't struggle if it wanted to. The surrendered wing rose once again and fell back. He raised the axe and, well-practised, swung it down. It hit the neck and immediately the head was off. The axe sank into the muck up to the handle. Blood gushed from the bird's neck as he pulled it free. The wing again fluttered. The eyes twitched open and shut. Vernon leaned down and from some instinct put his hand over the bird's eyes. The body stopped heaving.

He knew he'd done well but doubted the goodness of it. He stood, knees covered in a mix of gore and mud, and groaned.

Under his garden tap he washed the axe head clean, massaging it with his fingers, making sure not even a speck of muck remained to corrode it over time. He replaced it in the shed and padlocked the door. Then he resumed his seat, gazing out at the carcass of the bird. From this distance, the separation of head and body difficult to see. Maybe he'd done well.

~

Penelope arrived home. He heard her clomping through the house, dumping her handbag on the dining-room table, getting the kettle on. No lights on Snake Island yet. Rarely were nowadays. Kids had no sense of adventure. Nobody camped out there anymore.

'How was bowls?' he asked when she came out.

'Yeah, you know,' she said. 'What're you doing?'

'Just sitting,' he said, and nodded towards the pelican out on the flats. By now the tide had started to turn and there was water all around it. 'Had to kill a pelican.'

'Why?'

'It was dying out there. Choking on a plastic thing, from a six-pack.'

She leaned against the doorframe. 'It's the nineties. Haven't people seen the ads about littering?' She shifted her weight. 'So, did you shoot it?'

'I didn't shoot it. I used the axe.'

'And you're just going to leave it out there?'

He looked at it again, surrounded by the now floating seaweed.

'Well, what do you think, sweetheart?' he said.

'It'll attract sharks, won't it?'

He laughed at this. Looked at her for the first time. She was dressed in her bowling whites, sweating through her blouse. Nothing comical in her expression.

'You're not serious?'

'Won't it?'

'It won't attract bloody sharks.'

'You shouldn't just leave it, though. It's not proper.'

'No sharks down here anyway.'

'Yeah, there are. Old Paulie Westbrook caught one just the other day.'

'Oh, bullshit. Who said that?'

'Margie said. And watch your mouth.'

'Where, at bowls?'

'Yeah.'

'Paulie wouldn't've caught anything. Would've just said he did.'

'No, she said she saw it.'

'Lot of rubbish,' he said, and added a laugh for good measure. 'Where'd he say he caught it?'

'I don't know where. Nearby.'

He grunted. 'Paulie couldn't catch a cold without a jumper on.'

'So clever,' she said, folding her arms. 'You should've taken up comedy. Missed your calling in life teaching woodwork.'

He stood. Brushed at his muddied knees. 'Maybe out to sea there's gummies. But nothing comes down here. And who gives a damn anyway? They're not going to jump the rock wall and have a snap at you, are they?'

'Vernie . . .' she said.

She'd taken on that tone she had. He'd learned it well over the years. And knew, also, that were he to argue he'd be faced with her silence the remainder of the week. She had a way of needling him with it he couldn't shrug off. Probably because he should listen to her more often, and felt guilty for ignoring her.

Before he could respond, though, she re-entered the house. He heard the sound of the kettle being poured. He shouted, 'I'm not going out there and picking up that bird's corpse out of some strange sense of fear my wife has for sharks. It's not going to happen.'

She came back outside. 'Vernie. Come on. You can't just leave it.'

'I can.'

Soon, though, with the two of them seated beside one another, neither saying a word, and Pen sipping her tea without having made him any, he stood, grumbling, and gumbooted his feet. He unlocked the shed again and took from the wall his shovel. A slight, hurried anger in his actions, plain as day beneath his wife's gaze, he knew. The way he slammed the shed door. He saw within her eyes the hint of a smile as he climbed down the rock wall. Hard to tell if she was simply pleased he was doing what she'd asked, or if she found satisfaction in the power she held over him.

He splashed out to the bird. The briny smell had strengthened. The pelican's head had been washed away from the torso. He scanned the water for it but caught no sight of it. Absurdly, his wife's fear of sharks started to creep into him, so he was quick to lever the carcass onto his shovel and carry it stretched out before him back to the house. The weight of it difficult to carry in such a manner. It pinched between his shoulder blades. Too bloody old for this nonsense. He swore a bit as he walked towards his wife, lifting his gumboots out of the mud with stubborn determination. He stopped cursing as he neared her and offered her a forced smile. It made her smile in return all the same.

There was a patch of lawn at the rear of the garden that had always struggled to keep green grass, so he sat the headless bird there and started to dig. The work wasn't difficult but even so, his back grew sorer. Was a time this type of work had been easy. Now he resented the constant fight his body seemed to give the simplest task. Gardening, for any length of time. Bowling. Used to be he would have joined his wife for a game. Now his knees weren't up to the stress. His body at war with his spirit. Should have died in the bloody war, for all the good it's done me, he thought. Like Weymouth.

You old fool with your self-pity. He stopped his shovelling for a moment and in the low and dying light he looked at his wife, who was watching him. She raised her empty teacup in a gesture of unity. He remembered her in her youth as he watched her in the now. It was she that kept him going. He'd done that right, at least. Married the right woman. How long had it been since he'd thought that?

Soon the bird was in its hole. As he shovelled the dirt back in he heard a car on their driveway and his wife went in to greet the visitor. Strange to have one this time of evening. He was a sweaty, aching mess. Returning to the back porch, shovel washed and replaced in the shed, he collapsed onto his chair and stared with satisfaction at his job, and breathed happily.

The visitor rounded the corner and said, 'You need a beer, mate?'

'Too right I do.'

'You got some?'

'In the fridge.'

William Kelly returned with a stubby in each hand. He handed one to Vernon, in the stubby cooler Vernon had owned for years, then sat down in Penelope's chair. He gave a knowing look.

'What's she got you doing then?'

'Had to bury a dead pelican in the garden. Over there.' He motioned with his head. 'For fear of sharks.'

'No sharks'd swim up here.'

'I told her that.'

'You look an unholy mess.'

'I know.'

'Mmm,' Kelly said. He leaned forward, looked into the now knee-deep water, took a gulp of beer. 'You take your boat out much?' He gestured in the direction of Snake Island.

'No. Not really. Not for a bit. Haven't needed it.'

'Haven't needed the refuge?'

'Nah, mate. Nothing that bad has happened to me for going on a year now. Life's peachy.'

Kelly looked at the shed. 'How about the little one behind there?'

'With the oars?' Vernon grunted. 'Too old for that stupidity now.'

'You're right about that,' Kelly said, and added, 'I remember going out there with you when we were kids. What, fifty years ago?'

'Took Pen out there once. She hated it. Never took her again.'

'Don't get why you love it so much.'

'It's just dependable, I suppose. Always there. And everybody else seems to hate going out there, makes it easier to be alone.' He shifted, uncomfortable with where the conversation was heading. Then, 'Been a while since you come out here.'

'I know. I'm sorry about that. I might not look it but I feel like you look on the inside. Just a hell of a month, you know?'

'Yeah?'

'Yeah. A few funerals. Warren Bonner died. You remember him?'

'I knew him.'

'He served, too. You know that?'

'Always thought he was an arsehole.'

'Well. He was a bit.'

7

Vernon cleared his throat. The water now an inky black. The moon reflected. 'You ever think about it?'

'Dying?'

'The war.'

'I think about the war, sure. I think about dying more, though.'

Vernon remembered he'd thought of Weymouth earlier, but didn't want to bring him up. Didn't want to ever talk about him again, really. So he said, 'What do you think about?'

'I don't know. What it'll be like. Just, slipping away. How the Earth will function without me and how that's strange, you know? Stuff like that.'

'No doubts now you're so old about God and all that?'

Kelly laughed. 'Crummy line of work I got myself into if I doubted God.'

'How many times we had this discussion now?'

'Been having it a long time.'

'Just circling the same spot out of habit like a dog getting to bed?'

Kelly shrugged. Didn't offer a response.

Vernon said, 'So what did you come out here for then?'

Kelly looked at the newly covered hole in the earth and then down at his lap. He said, 'Saw your boy today.'

Vernon clenched his fist. He joined his friend in looking at the grave. Eventually he said, 'And?'

'He's not looking good, mate.'

'What do you mean he's not looking good?'

'You know how we take the choir out to the prison and sing a few carols round Christmas? Thought we'd do likewise for Easter this year, with a few hymns. So we went and sang. I kept an eye out for him but didn't see him. And some of the guards told me he wasn't good when I asked. So I went looking for him while we were on a break. They had him in the hospital bit.'

Vernon didn't move an inch.

'Well,' continued Kelly, 'he was banged up. Pretty bad. Had a dark bruise around his throat, like he'd been choked. Or tried hanging himself.'

'He deserves what he gets.'

Agony. Saying it. What he'd told himself he had to believe. Why he hadn't been out there to see his boy. Or help him. This *was* him helping, wasn't it? This discipline, this punishment. Let his son feel the weight of his crime. The pelican in the story letting those kids of hers grow up not being able to fend for themselves. Weakness. Molly-coddling. What would happen when she was dead, when they'd taken too much from her? They'd struggle, they'd die. His son would learn. His son would come good out of this. Such a rotten mess, though, the whole thing.

'You don't mean that, mate.'

Vernon looked away. 'I bloody do.'

Kelly sighed. 'Anyway, just thought you should know. He could probably do with a visit from you. Or Penelope. Or both of you.'

Vernon turned to regard his friend once more. 'We don't visit him. When he's done in there he's done and he can come back and be what-ever he wants to be, but we're not visiting him in there. He can bloody suffer for what he did and make amends for it that way. God knows, he won't do it out here.'

Kelly put his beer beside his chair and stood. He walked over to Vernon, sat on his haunches and in an act of intimacy put both hands on Vernon's hands. 'You have a think about what you just said to me. You have a think about all the things you've done in your life, and what it was like for you and your dad, and put yourself in your boy's position. I'm not going to preach scripture to you, 'cause I know you hate it, but you just think what it'd be like for you if you were in there and what you'd do to make amends. And have a think about what it'll be like for you when you're dying and this is how you did this.'

'Bloody alright. Get off me.'

Kelly went back to his chair and sipped at his beer. 'You have a think.'

'Get all bloody girly on me, mate.'

'You think about what you said.'

'Get off it. I will. Alright? Bloody hell.'

Penelope emerged, shoving open the sliding door. 'Can you two stop your swearing out here? You're not in the pub.'

'Sorry, Pen,' Kelly said.

'You should be sorry.'

'I wasn't swearing though!'

'Man of the cloth as you are.'

'I'm not in the vestments now.'

'You wear those robes even when you're not wearing them and you know it.'

He smiled. 'I should get going.' To Penelope he said, 'I just came to tell Vernon here about Caleb. I saw him today.'

Penelope's face curled in. 'We don't talk to him.'

'I know. Bit unlike you, though, Pen. Not sure how you live with it being that way.' He stood up once more and said, 'Thanks for the beer.'

'No problem,' Vernon said, but he didn't stand to see his friend out. Penelope did not walk him to the front door. He heard it shut gently and Penelope, her arms still folded, walked back into the kitchen. Vernon continued to stare at the grave and then stood and walked over. In the dark it appeared like concrete beside the textured grass. He scuffed his foot over it. They'd had an argument here. He and Caleb. About something stupid, something small, and Caleb had stormed indoors. Was there goodness in this world? It didn't seem there was. He sat down on his haunches and put his hands in the dirt.

~

Later that night, the two of them in bed, he turned to his wife, who had a *Woman's Weekly* in hand and her glasses on, and said, 'You want to hear what he had to say about Caleb?'

She didn't say anything and he watched her. What had he done to her, this kind woman, to make her so angry? Was it him? He was too afraid to ask. Soon she said, 'No. Thank you.'

'He's been hurt.'

'I said I didn't want to.'

Vernon sighed. Rolled onto his back and looked at the ceiling. 'I don't know what to do.'

'Well, you'll figure it out.'

'What would you do?'

'I'd shut up when my wife asked me to.'

He took a moment before he said, 'We've never really talked about it.'

She put her magazine down and placed her hands on it. When she spoke she was measured, calm. 'What do you want me to say?'

'I don't know. I suppose . . .'

'You want me to say I hate him?'

He just stared at her. He wondered at her emotionless voice.

'I don't know,' he eventually said.

She picked her magazine back up, flicked a page. 'I think about him every day, Vernie. Every day. And I picture her . . . Mel's face, you know? Her cheek, her nose. And I'm so ashamed of him. Everybody looks at me differently now.'

He nodded. 'Same with me.'

'It's not the same for you though, is it?' Another quick page turn. 'It's not the same. When a child does something well the man is praised for his success. When something happens . . . anyway. I don't need to get into all that. People *should* look at us different. That boy is our fault. What he did to Melissa . . . It might as well have been your hands around her throat.'

11

He kept watching her. He didn't understand how he had contributed to Caleb's crime but her words hit him square in the guts. That pelican sacrificing its blood to feed its young, dying in the process, wasting away while they prospered. What had he truly given up? He'd just left him in there. His son.

As she'd spoken there'd been no quaver in her voice, no water in her eyes. A deep and unclimbable chasm between them and all she would do was stare at it, it seemed. And walk away. From him. He turned his light off and shut his eyes, her light still ebbing its way into his consciousness. She did not bury herself into him the way she used to. That chasm. They'd never climb out of it.

TWO

~

CALEB MOORE

A thought clawing at him. One he didn't want to entertain. Behind his eyes, right there. A cat wanting to get at him, scratching at a door. A constant thing. He did his best to ignore it but it was always there. He should let it in, really. He deserved to be hurt. But the few times he had let it in he'd almost killed himself. Sitting there with the razor blade staring at him. Too much of a wimp to even remove it from the packet.

The lot of them in front of him, kicking the footy around, kicking up dust: fellow prisoners garbed in muddy white. He'd finally been cleared to re-enter the normal rhythm of the prison after his stint in the hospital wing, so he sat watching. Trying not to think too hard on what he'd done. The same battle he'd faced the entirety of his sentence.

Her face. When he'd struck her he hadn't been right in the head. He'd come home from a hard day and she'd just been at him about something. And then his mind had left his body. The red mist, he'd heard it called. It hurt him, what she'd said, and he'd reacted.

Utter rot. He'd hit her countless times. On multiple occasions. And been told off by the police. And done it again. And been locked up a

13

few days. Repentance, sorrow when he got home. On his knees more than once, crying, running his hands over her bruises. Got a few beers in, the mates egging him on, his own insecurities and failures; the cycle born anew. She wouldn't even need to say anything. Just look at him. And it was all her fault? You best accept you did it. You best accept and live with it. Was nothing to do with her. Was everything broken in you. You live with it. The least you can do.

He scuffed at the dirt with his foot. Quit making excuses. Do what Reverend Kelly said. One of the blokes grabbed the ball and wheeled it about, showing off, being a tosser. Another shouldered into him, too rough. The boys were all soon shoving each other, throwing punches. Two guards walked in yelling, telling them to calm down, telling them they'd be locked in their rooms, no more exercise for them. Caleb only watched.

What he wouldn't do to take it back. His hands around her throat. Some part of him stopping before he killed her. But he could have. Could have wrenched her spirit from her body.

There'd been no intention in what he'd done. In the midst of it there had been that other part of him, screaming at him. Watching his actions from behind a barrier. Like his body was fuelled by something else, another soul, just for that moment. And he'd watched her eyes bulge, watched her anger turn to fear, turn to terror. He was bigger than her, much bigger. In that moment he'd stolen something from her. The noise she'd made. This was after he'd scarred her face, smashed her nose. He grimaced now remembering it, still watching the fight breaking up, the boys resuming their game. The dust rising up behind the football. He'd never forget that noise.

Thank God he'd stopped. She'd been right to press charges and get them to stick that final time. Right to divorce him.

The prisoner sitting beside him was too close for Caleb's liking. He moved over to allow the man more room.

'You ever wanna run?' the bloke said. He turned to look at Caleb, squinting in the sun. He nodded towards the tree line beyond the field.

'Every second,' Caleb said. 'Every bloody second.'

'Hard not to,' he said. 'It's right there.'

'They'd catch you. Then extend your sentence another twelve months, send you someplace else.'

'I know. They gave us the lecture.'

Caleb sighed. 'You new, then?'

'What you think? You seen me before?'

'Alright. Bloody hell.'

The man looked apologetic. 'Got here two days ago. They said 'cause I been good they were sending me here for the last six months. I don't know. I don't know how good I been.'

Caleb willed the man to leave. The sun was setting slowly, bleeding out over the clouds. The men and their game would soon be cleared.

'You going to play?' the man asked.

'No,' Caleb said.

'Why not?'

'Don't deserve to.'

The man laughed, the sound cruel. 'You a poof?'

The man's laughter died when he saw Caleb would not respond and he stood and walked into the game, shouting about not getting a touch, pointing back at Caleb on the bench, the word *faggot* piercing the air.

As he watched the bloke expertly claim the ball, Caleb thought of his father. He'd taught Caleb how to kick. He'd been patient and able. Hold both hands on top, mate, that's it. Look where you want the ball to go and make sure both hands are out straight, like that. Lean forward, over it. The gruff determination. Caleb felt the sun go down. Soon he was rounded up, sent back to his room. Lying on his bunk again.

~

15

The next day Caleb was at breakfast with the others when the governor stood up in front of them. He was a weak-looking man, pudgy
around his arms. A weak-looking man unable to stand up to the
Cahills. Hard to blame him, really. Still, hard not to hate him either.

'We've been leading up to our Prisoners on the Run event for a bit
now, so you blokes should be used to this speech, but I gotta give it
again for the new blokes.'

The man Caleb had been speaking to the day before put his hand
up and said, 'You letting us all go then, mate?'

The governor's voice rose above the din. 'This is a special charity
event we do each year. You only get to come if you've been on your
best behaviour. We gotta be able to trust you. We take all of you out
onto the road and go for a bit of a jog.'

Daryl, from the back: 'Like to see you jog, copper.'

Nobody laughed this time.

The governor said, 'Hear the lack of laughter there, Daryl? I can
let one joke go, but you keep disrespecting me . . .' He looked at the
man. The governor shifty before them all, like he saw within them the
makings of an uprising. Trying to muster his courage, plain for all to
see. Hitching his pants up, sticking his neck out. 'You won't be going
at this rate, yeah? You treat us with respect like you know how—you
wouldn't be here otherwise—and you'll go.'

The governor let his eyes rest on Caleb a moment too long. Then
he said, 'Right. Finish your breakfast, everybody. We'll do some exercise after.'

The men groaned, the wailing of cattle led to the slaughter.

'Now, now,' the governor shouted. 'You be good about it we'll let
you play another game after, same as yesterday.'

The groaning soon subsided. As the governor reached the door he
looked back at Caleb, his mouth gripped tight. Then he turned and let
them be.

Later Caleb was on his bed, staring at the ceiling, doing his best to keep his thoughts at bay, focusing instead on the weatherboards, the sound of the plumbing in another room. Ignoring the sound of her in his mind.

The beating that had led to the bruise around his neck, the marks across his chest, his aching leg had happened over a week ago. Brendan Cahill had shown up one day out of the blue, striding into his room. Paid off or intimidated the governor. Brendan had never liked him at school, and was still acting like he owned the joint, the way Caleb remembered. Sauntering in with a cricket bat, though he hadn't used it. Just threatened with it, shouting, thudding it against the walls. Asking Caleb if he knew why he'd come. Caleb still had no idea. Instead of the bat he'd used his fists, relishing the sound they made as they struck Caleb. Caleb wasn't guessing; Brendan had told him, bragged about it.

Thing was, Caleb deserved it. Maybe Brendan was God striking him, pummelling him, making his flesh purple and yellow, green as it healed. Maybe it was God raising his cheeks up, swelling the left eye until it was just a slit through which he couldn't see. Retribution from on high.

Now he was sitting on his bed just waiting. That was the worst of it. Brendan had said he'd be back. Hadn't said when. The door unlocked. The unguarded forest just near. Some fellas had run off only months before. They'd been caught. They were all caught eventually.

This fear, though? Same thing he'd done to her. Same exact thing. Melissa waiting at home for him to return, probably feeling this same terror. Hoping that he'd changed. Despair when she heard his angry footsteps. When she saw his eyes.

He stared at the ceiling, rubbed at his own eyes. Where was the evil born in you? Dad had been Dad. He'd been alright. Never struck him, nothing beyond a smack. Never struck their mother. He hadn't been exactly kind, though. Just a numb type of anger whenever Caleb got something wrong. That or complete apathy. One of those dads who sat in the car the duration of their son's footy game instead of

'The trick is,' he said, 'you gotta be careful and calm. And get their heads right off quick. You gotta hold 'em, too. Upside down, let the blood out. Hope they don't wriggle free.' His calm voice mollifying Daisy. 'They don't know they're dead for a bit. Their body kicks around. Walking around like nothing's happened.'

He petted her. Her brown chook. The dull yellow of her talons. The dopey manner. He lowered her into the dust, the chook too stupid to try escaping. With a quick motion he raised the tomahawk and brought it down, almost softly. The head came free instantly, rolled over like a marble, gathering sticky dust. He held the body in the crook of his arm against his shirt. He stood. He turned the body upside down but as he did so the wings came loose and started flapping. His grip weakened. He grabbed at her but she was slipping, headless, dripping muck from the neck. Soon her wings were entirely free, flapping erratically, all sense to the motion gone with the head. Her father's face slowly mottled with red. He held his arms out straight, having lost all hope of control. The headless bird swung free, kicking, throbbing, butting into the fence.

Sharon stepped back. The blood covering her father's arms. Leaking like a tap turned on full blast. She watched, amazed at the amount. Daisy in her death painting her father his truer shade.

~

They looked like her chickens. When she'd been young, she would walk through the coop trailing pellets, letting them drip from her hand, and they had crowded around her ankles, bowling one another over in their haste. Her three police officers were milling in the same manner, bumping shoulders, laughing, wanting to get at the cake.

Sharon leaned over the cake, which she hadn't made herself. She hadn't had time to make anything, just bought it at Freddie's. She looked at the other pub patrons, happily ignoring the policemen. She lowered the knife, sliced into the frosting.

Jack, the youngest by far, held out a napkin-covered hand, expecting the first slice.

'Proper manners'd say Rob gets first piece, being the oldest,' Sharon said. She levered the slice onto the blade.

'I don't mind, Sharon,' Robert said, but accepted the proffered cake anyway. Jack kept on looking, waiting his turn.

Trevor, a middle-aged bloke with a huge gut, next to Jack, said, 'Why're we here again?'

'We're starting a new Easter tradition. We're going to be busy the day of Prisoners on the Run and the Boolarra Festival. So we're having chocolate cake and beer now.'

Trevor said, 'Doesn't sound like something we'd do.'

'For Easter,' she repeated, giving Trev his slice.

He started eating immediately. 'What do you mean? We don't normally do this stuff.' Spitting crumbs.

'Yeah,' Jack said. 'We don't even celebrate Christmas together.'

'Well, all that's changing.'

'We'll hold you to that,' Jack said, raising his piece of cake like he was toasting their good fortune.

'So,' she said, 'you boys want a beer?'

She went to the bar, ordered four beers. Previously she'd managed to distract them from Ernie's activities with callouts, assignments. Last time she'd had them sorting boxes of old files, putting them in a new filing cabinet she'd bought. Completely useless work. Made her anxious and guilty, conning them like that. This was better. At least this way they were happy. As she turned to carry the beers back Jack dashed up beside her, taking two from her crowded hands, offering his apologetic smile.

As she sat back down, Trevor said, 'I like it. Nice to be out, talking, not wearing the uniform.'

'While I appreciate this whole thing, Sharon,' Robert said, 'I'm not sure it's such a good idea. It leaves the town without police.'

'It's Newbury,' Sharon said. 'What's going to happen?'

'You never know.'

'Nothing ever happens.'

'When I was first a policemen here—' Robert said.

'Tell what it was like when those kids were kidnapped,' Jack interrupted.

Robert took a moment. 'No, I've told that one to death. This one I don't think I've ever told anybody. I was around twenty years old. Yeah, I would've been. And one of my first callouts.' He swallowed. 'I went down by the prison, but it wasn't a prison back then.'

'What was it?'

'It wasn't anything back then. Was just an empty paddock. But it was around the area, you know. I was only twenty, I think. I was called down there because boys had been throwing rocks at cars.'

'How old were you then?'

Robert laughed. 'You bugger.'

Sharon said, 'What year was this?'

'Would have been the mid-sixties, I think. Maybe late sixties,' Robert finished his cake. Dabbed at the corners of his mouth with his handkerchief, enjoying the attention, however sarcastic it might be.

'They were throwing rocks at cars. Just being kids. As I drove up I could see smoke. I went over the hill and saw a car smashed into a tree. Really banged up. The whole front crumpled in on itself like a sandwich. You ever seen a crash like that?'

All three nodded.

'Then you know what it's like. Going up to the car.'

'What did you do?' Jack said.

'Well, I went up to the car and my first thought is there are probably dead people inside. And I was just new on the job. So I hesitated a little. By myself, you understand? Just the first on the scene. But I radioed back and then I found my legs a bit and walked up to the car. And there was a couple in there. She was crying, he was knocked out. There was blood. He looked dead, is what I first thought. So I went to him and found his pulse and pulled him from the car while she's screaming about her kid.'

'Was there a kid in the back?' Sharon asked.

'Turned out she was pregnant. She lost that kid, was the thing of it. Yeah,' he said, not meeting their eyes. 'So I think about me hesitating on approach and what those moments could've meant to that little kid in there.'

'The crash probably killed it on impact,' Jack said.

Robert breathed in, leaned back. 'So I'm saying things do happen in Newbury. Sometimes they do.'

'It wouldn't've mattered, you being there quickly,' Sharon said. 'A couple minutes more wouldn't've made a difference.'

'You never know, though, do you? I got her out quick.'

'We're just a phone call away if something happens tonight.'

'I know, I know. But we're all drinking a bit. We're not alert. Next time—I'm just saying—one of us should be at the station.'

Sharon looked at her police force, saw Robert's story had done its job. And well it should. Her reasons for keeping them at the pub were shameful. She wanted to do it right, for once, tell them to head out to the spot where the Cahills traded their weed. Arrest them. Lock them up. To hell with the consequences. She'd taken beatings.

Instead she said, 'Well, that wouldn't be exactly fair.'

'I'd do it.'

Sharon finished her beer. Looked at the others' pints, still nearly full.

Trevor said, 'What happened to them anyway? The woman? The bloke in the car?'

'Well, I got them on the ground and the ambulance came. You know how crashes work.'

'Was the bloke alive?'

'Oh yeah, he come to pretty quick. She was okay too, in the end, besides the baby. Just a bad dust-up.'

Jack said, 'What about the kids?'

Robert looked serious. 'What kids are you talking about? They didn't have any other kids.'

'The kids throwing rocks.'

'Oh, them. Never found 'em. No idea about them.'

'But wasn't that why they crashed?'

Robert tilted his head. 'For the life of me, you know, I can't remember.'

'Come on.'

'I can't remember. This is going back thirty-odd years now. You remember what happened thirty years ago when you hit my age and I'll buy you the beer.'

'You'll be bloody dead by then,' Trevor said.

Sharon went to the bar with her empty glass and when the publican looked at her she nodded and was soon greeted with a full pint, froth sloshing over the side. As she turned, instead of immediately walking back she watched the men, the two too young and the one too old. Even Robert was enjoying himself. But she had only taken them out tonight because of Ernie Cahill. Try as she might there was no way she could enjoy herself.

TEN

~

SIDNEY CAHILL

The back roads of Newbury ran through large pastures, blankets of empty dark, sporadic trees lonely against the starry horizon. As he drove the headlights shone on fenceposts and old farmsteads. One was dilapidated, had been since Sidney could remember. He had played with his brother there until their mother found them out. They'd ducked in between fence palings. Brendan would sometimes use them as cricket bats and Sidney would throw clods of dirt and cow pats at him, which he fended with a skill Sidney envied. It was always just the two of them when they were little. Even after Brendan found his friends he still didn't bring them out here. As the headlights struck it there was only shadow, all definition lost in the ghostly light.

He turned the corner and arrived at the drop-off point. Down an old dirt road for a kilometre. He slowed the car and stopped it beside a tree. He turned off the lights. Melbourne had chosen this spot because it was only ten minutes from town, but any old bugger from Newbury or Devonshire or Trenton knew this spot. Melbourne, in their arrogance, didn't care about his father's protests.

He sat. With the radio off he was surrounded by darkness and little else. He wound his window down and breathed in the country air, full of cow manure and hay. He loved this smell. Most of his thoughts were centred on his daughter. He wondered when she would start walking. She'd taken a few small steps already, but had tripped over. He'd tried once to push her on. It had ended up making her cry. They'd been in the kitchen and she had stood up and he'd held out his arms and cooed and sweet-talked her, but her bottom lip had dropped and she'd cried to be picked up. He hadn't, though. He'd kept on talking to her, urging her forward. Come on there bubba, there's a girl. That's the way, that's it, Amy. Keep going. She hadn't taken a step, crying for around three minutes, wobbling on her feet, and finally fell heavily on her front, smacking her lips and teeth on the floor, splaying her arms outward. He still felt bad about it.

Sooner than he'd expected, headlights announced a car at the turn-off down the dirt road. Sidney checked his watch. Brendan had been right. Early buggers. They crept forwards slowly. Sidney looked at the glovebox. Out the window he noticed a kangaroo behind trees. It was munching on grass as the car approached, the beams reflected in its gaze so that it too appeared alien, monstrous. It was a big bastard.

The car stopped before him, about two lengths in front. Its head-lights winked out. For a moment nothing happened. Then Sidney heard a door open, and footsteps on the dirt. He opened his own door, unbuckled his seatbelt, and got out, the breeze instantly freezing. He shut the door.

'You Melbourne?' he asked.

The figure did not respond and in that moment Sidney knew he was in trouble. Then he saw the barrel of a rifle—or was it a shot-gun?—dangled against the figure's leg.

'I'm not Melbourne,' he said. 'Get back in your car.'

'Who are you?'

The gun was lifted and pointed at his chest.

'Car.'

'Alright, alright,' Sidney said. He raised his arms and stepped towards his car. 'Can I open the door?'

'Bloody get bloody in the car, mate. And sit there.'

Sidney opened the door carefully and slumped in without the aid of his hands. The figure in the dark walked around to the other side of the car and tried the handle, found the door locked. He tapped patiently on the window with the butt of the shotgun. Sidney leaned over and flicked up the lock. The man opened the door and got in.

Sidney put both hands on the steering wheel.

'What's your name?' the man asked. 'You Sidney?'

'Who are you?'

'Are you the one hitting my boy?' The man shifted in the seat so that the shotgun was resting on his lap and pointing right at Sidney's thigh. 'Or you the other one?'

'I'm Sidney. I don't know what you're on about.'

'Right. You're the other one.'

'What are you doing?'

'You drive home, then.'

'What, with you in here?'

The old man nodded. In the difficult light Sidney could now almost see his face and it was weathered and firm. No hint of panic. 'I want you to drive home.'

'You know who I am?'

'You just said you were Sidney.'

'Sidney Cahill.'

'Yeah.'

'But do you know who I am?'

'You just bloody said that, mate. Get the car started.'

'I mean, do you know who my dad is?'

'I imagine he's old Ernie Cahill.' The old man lifted the barrel of the shotgun slightly. 'Have you noticed I have a gun on you?'

'You're not going to shoot me.'

78

'Just start the car, would you?'

Sidney fumbled, had to lift his arse from the seat to get the keys from his pocket.

'What're you doing?' the old man said.

'Getting the keys out.'

'Bloody hell.'

Sidney stuck them in the ignition and the engine turned over. The car sprang to life, the headlights illuminating the old man's car in front of his. If he'd had his headlights on Sidney would've seen the shabbiness of the vehicle. Plain as day he wasn't from Melbourne.

'You sure you want to do this?'

The old man leaned back again. 'I'm sure.'

'Knowing who my old man is?'

'We established this already.'

'Knowing what he'll do to you?'

'He won't do anything to me.'

'You know why I'm out here?'

The old man lifted his head from the headrest and stared at Sidney. 'I imagine something nefarious.'

'Something nefarious? What's that?'

'I'm not an idiot. I didn't just stumble onto you out here in the dark, sitting in your car. I know why you're here.'

'My old man is going to kill you.'

'He won't,' the old man said.

'I'm just watching out for you.'

He grunted, clearly fed up. 'Start the car.'

'It's already started.'

'I mean put it in bloody gear and drive home, like I asked.'

Sidney looked down the end of the road, hoping somebody would show. Nobody did. He put the car in first and crunched down the dirt, the old man's shotgun trained on his legs.

Sidney risked the occasional glance and noticed this man was quite relaxed, despite all that was ahead of him. He was wearing the clothes of the elderly, had his white hair combed. Looked like he was maybe seventy, an old sixty.

Sidney said, as they rounded another corner. 'What do you want?'

'I told you what I want.'

'No, you didn't.'

The old man grunted, sat up a bit. 'Your brother Brendan has been beating my boy up. I'm going to get him to stop.'

Sidney took a moment, looked at the fence as he travelled beside it. Looked again at the shed he and his brother used to muck around in as it grew smaller in the rearview mirror. 'This won't help. This won't stop Brendan. It'll just make him dig his heels in further, keep on doing whatever he's doing.'

'I'm not going to talk to Brendan. I'm going to talk to your dad.'

'This won't help with Dad, either.'

'Well,' the old man said, 'I reckon I don't give a shit. I have a shotgun and I have you.'

Sidney shook his head, raised his shoulders, tried to look annoyed. Bloody Brendan and his impulses. Wasn't the first time he'd landed them in trouble. Sidney didn't doubt for a second that the old man's grievances were justified.

'So what was I going to do?' the old man said. 'Go to the cops? Sharon Wornkin? She's worse than your old man. In your old man's pocket. So what could I do? You tell me.'

Sidney shrugged again.

'You know how bloody rude that is, just shrugging like that?'

'You have a shotgun pointed at my leg, so maybe don't lecture me on manners.'

This made the old man laugh. 'Have a bit of respect, mate. At least respect the gun,' he said, and hefted it. Looked out the window. 'I'm going to try to appeal to your dad's sense of being a dad. A father, you know, like me.'

'He won't much like you having a shotgun on me.'

The old man did nothing for a moment and then he removed the shotgun from his lap and laid it on the floor of the backseat, in front of all the boxes of tomato paste jars full of weed. 'There.'

'You're trusting.'

'Not really.'

Sidney thought of his daughter again and what he would do if she were threatened and he knew that this man beside him was exercising restraint; that he, Sidney, would not be so reserved, that he would be right in the face of whoever was doing harm to Amy and he would not just be holding a bloody gun, he'd be pulling the trigger and reloading the shells and pulling it again until he was out of ammunition. The violence he felt at the mere thought was enough to make Sidney sympathise. He looked again at the old man and understood what was making him tick. He knew what he aimed to do and was confident his intentions were good, despite the gun, despite being on the end of it.

They passed a stone memorial on their left that Sidney had never stopped to properly look at. As they rounded a bend a kangaroo stared at them in the headlights from the side of the road. Sidney slowed as they passed and the kangaroo flicked its ears and he kept on. He sped up without noticing the kangaroo on the opposite side of the road. The sound of the engine revving startled it into action and before he was able to nudge at the brakes it bounded in front of them.

Both men were slammed forwards. Sidney's face smashed into the dashboard. The kangaroo, limbs flailing, collided with the windscreen. There was a cacophony of destroyed glass. He was thrown back and surrounded by shrieking, half of it from him. The old man was gone, swallowed in the chaos. All Sidney could see was fur and all he could smell was animal. He'd somehow managed to slam on the brakes. The car swerved and screeched. The kangaroo was still alive. It clawed and thrummed its legs at Sidney's chest through the space where the windscreen had been. He knew his chest was gashed by its claws. He tried to look, to not look. He pushed back at it, hands sticky with blood. No telling where the creature's head was, what were its legs. He just felt a whirring like a chainsaw against his arm, the left, his chest. He fought again breath.

The car stopped and the animal kept kicking. Sporadic, seconds between thrums. Sidney breathed and fought against his weakness but knew the animal had him pinned. Somehow, though, it soon fell off him, out of the car. He slumped back into his seat and looked at the roof of the car and looked at his hand smeared with red. Amy—the last thought clear in his head before he forgot everything.

ELEVEN

~

VERNON MOORE

The kid stopped speaking and instead seemed to concentrate all his energy on driving. His hands fixed to the wheel, gripping it hard. Both hands. Like he was still learning. Ten and two o'clock. Vernon remembered briefly teaching Caleb. The kid—Sidney, he said his name was—was going a bit fast round the bends considering the poor traction on the dirt, but Vernon was giving him the benefit of the doubt. Had driven it thousands of times probably. The gun on the floor behind was small comfort but he knew now the kid was unarmed, would have reached for something if he had it. The car was a dump, full of boxes and mess, old cling wrap scrunched up and thrown in balls near his feet.

Vernon shifted his weight in the seat. He didn't want violence. Just an audience. Just a sit-down, man to man, with Ernie. He wouldn't even bring the gun in. Just the kid.

They rounded a bend and Vernon saw the kangaroos, saw a lot of them munching their grass, saw one of them bound towards the car. The kid, in that instant, was looking in the other direction and Vernon saw the collision before it happened. He managed to duck before the car slammed into the kangaroo, his arms braced against the dashboard for impact. The thunderous smash of glass and the grunting of the animal and the swerving of the car. Vernon held onto the door handle with one hand, put the other on the handbrake. The kid was being pummelled. The massive hind legs of the animal were cartwheeling against his chest and in the dark with his head back and his mouth open he was screaming like a child. As the car slowed, Vernon opened his door, the kangaroo's tail smacking into his head. He fell with an awkward thud onto the dirt. It didn't take long for the car to stop completely.

He levered himself up and hobbled as quick as he could to the front of the car, his old knees aching. The kangaroo was still on the bonnet. One of its eyes was bulging out, almost out of the socket. He grabbed at its fur and pushed it off the car. It was so impaled in the metal he had to lift it a bit. It flopped onto the dirt and lay there kicking, its tail rigid, quaking, its eyes unseeing. Just black glossy dots amid the mess. Its legs were all bent.

He looked through the smashed windshield and saw the kid in there breathing in big hurried gasps. There was blood coating his chest, soaking his flannel shirt so that it was reflective like the eye of the roo. No moonlight in the car though. His eyes were shut in a grimace, his teeth bared. But he was breathing.

Vernon opened the door and the kid fell onto the road, stirring dust, jarring his arm. He didn't speak. Maybe he was unconscious. 'Mate?' Vernon asked, and flipped him onto his back. 'You alright?'

The kid didn't answer, holding his arm to his chest, moaning.

'Let me look, mate.'

Vernon tried to move the arm but found it gripped there with a strength he had not guessed at in the kid. He tried to coax it and was reminded of the war. The kid held it steady.

From his position he looked at the roo. Its legs had slowed, but it was still grunting, breathing hurried like the kid. It would be in pain.

When he came to the cemetery he stood a moment with his elbows propped on the fence and regarded the stones and thought of all the people buried there, skeletons in the earth, and thought what it would be like if they were to rise from their graves and come for him in the dark with their arms outstretched. Or if they'd walk at all, or float like spectres, and he thought of all those he'd known who were now dead, all who'd perished in the war, and old Barney his boss who had died on the job, teaching kids, supervising, a heart attack as he pointed to the flower parts on the blackboard, noting the stamen. How he'd fallen. Even Vernon in the building nearby heard the sound of his body colliding with the laminate. Dead, skeletal now, all of them. Weymouth in the ground. His one good eye forever staring straight into Vernon. Who would be dead too, eventually. Though would he know it then? His son in there with him too, all of them, every person, every son, every daughter. Dead for certain. What was the point? If nothing mattered then nothing bloody mattered and he might as well just lie down in an open grave here now and let nature do its work.

~

Back home he opened his front door, his back dripping sweat after his effort, the night breeze cooling it against his skin. He prised his boots off as he walked inside, tiptoed over the carpet. The laundry taps provided him with water so that his wife wouldn't hear.

It took him what seemed a full minute to shut the bedroom door. Holding the handle down, moving it in millimetres, then creeping over to the bed, removing his clothes, wincing as they rustled.

'Don't bother with all the silence.'

'Bloody hell.'

'You think I can fall asleep with you out God-knows-where?'

She flicked her light on and sat up and looked at her husband with all the derision and anger he knew she felt.

'Come on, I told you where I was.'

'You said you were going to find the Cahill boy and talk some sense into him, which means God-knows.'

'Stop saying that.'

'And you took the gun,' she said. Then he saw it, in the dark: real hurt in her face. She was maybe crying, maybe had earlier in the night. Normally their arguments did not extend past annoyance. And she didn't cry.

'How do you know that?' he asked, regretting the question the minute it left him.

'You left the back shed door open.'

'No, I didn't.'

'Well, it was open when I looked out there, and I walked in and the gun was gone. Are you gonna tell me what you were thinking?' She was near tears and it made him hurt. 'What *were* you thinking, Vernie? What were you *doing*?'

He tried to shush her, cooing at her like she was pigeon, but her arms were crossed and his cooing only seemed to strengthen her resolve. He sat on the bed beside her and looked at his hands. 'I'm sorry.'

'Sorry is nothing. Sorry's a rotten word.'

'I know,' he said, and then, 'I was just going to scare him a bit.'

She snorted. 'Scare him a bit. He's a Cahill, Vernie. They don't scare at guns.'

'He'd been hitting my boy.'

'He's my boy too.'

'Well, he'd been hitting him. I'm not going to go in there with my shoulders all slumped and ask him pretty please will you stop. People like that only understand power.'

She said nothing for a moment. Then, 'Did it work?'

'I don't know.'

'Did you talk to them?'

'I talked to Ernie and he seemed to agree to get it stopped. Seemed like he didn't know it was happening. It was his oldest, Brendan.'

'Did you take the shotgun in?'

He nodded. 'But I had it down. Just so they knew I was serious.'

'And they weren't mad?'

'Well. Ernie was a bit.'

'But he said he'd have it stopped?'

'That's what he said.'

She finally unfolded her arms but drew no closer to her husband. She said, 'I thought I might go and visit him tomorrow.'

'Ernie?'

'Get off it,' she said. 'Caleb.'

'Yeah?'

'Just take him some things.'

Vernon looked at the ceiling. 'I regret it. Not going to visit him before this. You should have seen him.'

'You said.'

'Don't you regret it?'

In the dark her face was unknowable. 'I always regretted it.'

She shuffled onto her back and rolled from him, bunching the sheets around her, flicking off her light. He said nothing else and in their now shadowed ceiling he conjured up the image of the cemetery, the concrete headstones, what it would be like to regard so many dead from above, or below. He thought of how his wife had spoken of their son since he beat Mel. Her words now. Had she really regretted it? Had she forgiven their son? He sat there on their bed staring at her back.

FIFTEEN

~

SHARON WORNKIN

The next morning Sharon woke late. She turned over, saw that Roger's side of the bed was still made up. His digital clock said nine o'clock. Did she have to work today? She sat upright. Remembered what had happened the previous night. Held her face in her hands. Groaned. She had to go in later. That's right. Afternoon shift.

She changed into her exercise clothes—loose fitting, so she didn't feel too self-conscious—and slumped into the living room. All her joints ached with drink, with effort. Was she hungover? She hadn't drunk that much? She turned the television on and inserted a VHS tape of *Aerobics Oz Style*. She hit 'play' on the remote and a woman, bright and cheery, coaxed her onwards. Sharon had never met a person in real life with a smile like that. The exercises never made her feel fit, but did make her feel better, like she was working towards something.

Afterwards, in the shower, she started crying. She soaped herself and rinsed and soaped again. Last night she hadn't done the right thing. Roger would say she had. That she'd preserved herself, their relationship with Ernie. That it was important. But she should've acted. Stepped up. Drawn her weapon. If she'd had her weapon. Smashed their noses in with it. Let them bleed onto the soggy carpet. Let the locals witness what it meant to harm one of hers.

She sank to the floor of the shower recess and put her face on the white tiles and breathed, watching her breath make ripples that quickly dispersed. She hadn't done a thing as her father had lopped Daisy's head off. As Ernie had damn near ripped his son's head off. Never stood up for a damn thing, ever.

When she entered the kitchen her son was at the bench eating Coco Pops and reading a guitar magazine. Sharon was still towelling her hair. Coco Pops hadn't been her intention, but she found herself grabbing a bowl and pouring milk.

'You were out late last night?' she said to Peter.

He didn't look up. 'I was right here. You were the one who was out late.'

She couldn't tell if his inattention was forced or accidental.

'What're you up to today?' she said.

'Don't know. Might go see Cassie later.'

'Yeah? And do what?'

'Don't know. What about you?' Peter asked, still not looking at her.

'Not sure, yet.'

'You have the day off?'

She remembered what she'd promised to do last night. It made her angry at herself, at Ernie for having asked. She wondered if Cassie knew, how much Peter knew about what went on out there.

'I have to go in later.'

Peter looked up finally. 'What does that mean?'

'I've got the afternoon shift. And there's something I have to take care of. Probably be out late tonight with it.'

'With what?'

Lying to her own son. 'Some old bloke at Port Napier stole a car last night.' She poured more milk into her bowl, as if to cover her shame. While she chewed she asked, 'Did you hear what else happened last night? Down at the pub?'

'Cassie said something on the phone about it this morning. Said there were two blokes you took out to their place. From Melbourne?'

'Yeah,' Sharon said. 'She didn't say anything else?'

'No. Should she have?'

Sharon thought about the way she imagined the locals had looked at her as she left the pub. That they'd all known what she was. With a horror she'd never before felt she realised that her son now wore the same expression.

'I guess not,' she finally said. 'What do you think of all that?'

'Of all what?'

'Of what the Cahills do?'

'What do the Cahills do?'

Sharon took another mouthful as she thought about how to put it nicely. 'With the fellas from Melbourne.'

'Who were they?'

'Cassie doesn't talk to you about it?'

'No.'

By now her son had stopped eating. Sharon put her own spoon down.

'Forget it,' she said.

'No. What do they do?'

'Just forget it, sweetheart. I'm sorry, I shouldn't've brought it up.'

Peter looked for a moment like he might continue his questions, but instead picked up his spoon again and turned back to his magazine.

'They're not anybody. They're just friends of Ernie's.'

'Yeah, alright, Mum.'

'Well, they are. They were just getting drunk a bit and I wanted to know what you thought of that, getting drunk . . .' Bloody hell, her words sounded strained. Not even she would buy what she was trying to sell. 'You're eighteen now, you know? I wanted to know what you thought.'

'You told me to leave it and I'm leaving it, alright?'

He didn't look up. Refilled his bowl with Coco Pops. Amazing to her how much he could eat. She remembered feeding him Coco Pops when he'd been, what, three? Every spoonful into his mouth just so. She remembered him sneezing once, and small brown globs pasting her shirt, the two of them laughing. The guitar magazine now holding his attention. His clouded eyes. He said nothing more to her. She sat watching her son in muted desperation, ashamed of her lies, every one of them burning holes in her gut.

SIXTEEN

~

VERNON MOORE

Near midday when he finally woke. He scrunched his hands into a fist and rubbed at his eyes. There was a sickness in the back of his throat.

He swung his legs around to rest on the floor and was met with an almighty pain shooting down both calves. He rocked back and winced and sucked in air through his teeth. His knees felt like they'd collapse beneath the weight of him. These bloody knees. He pulled his toes back as far as he could, stretching out the muscle. Probably hadn't walked as far since his army days. Never any need for it.

He sat on the bed a bit and then, to his surprise, his wife appeared in the doorway.

'You're awake at last.' She regarded him. 'Are you in pain?'

He nodded. 'Legs hurt.'

'Why?'

He stared a moment before saying, 'You going out?'

'I've been out. Got some groceries.'

'Did you get the ham? For the Easter thing with my brother?'

'We're going to that?' she asked.

'We're not?'

'We didn't talk about it.'

'We always go.'

'I know, but with things with Caleb . . .'

He turned away from her, massaged his calves.

She said, 'Where's your car?'

'What?'

'Our other car? *Your* car.'

He turned back to her. 'You want to spend Easter with Caleb now?'

She nodded, slow and thoughtful. So. He'd maybe helped, maybe given her permission to reconnect. Done something good. If there was such a thing.

She said, 'I thought we could. This year. Might be nice for him. Stop avoiding the question. Where's the car?'

'He's doing that run thing, though.'

'After that, I thought. Vernon, where's your car?'

'I had to leave it.'

'Where?'

'Can we continue this in the kitchen? I want to get something to eat.'

At the kitchen counter she stood on the opposite side to him with both hands palms down. He felt the separation between them. Out the window was Snake Island. His escape. It'd be so easy to head out there. Get in the boat and just go.

He put bread in the toaster, got out the butter and Vegemite and looked at her while he waited for his toast to spring.

'I had to leave the car. It got smashed.'

'Smashed how?'

'We hit a kangaroo.'

'In the car? Who's "we"?'

'Yes, in the car,' he said. He looked at the toaster. 'Well, our car didn't hit it.'

129

'Would you just bloody tell me what happened?' she said, tapping her hands on the benchtop. 'And don't lie to me, Vernie. I can tell when you're keeping stuff from me, you know I can.'

'Well, like Margie said, they were down that old dirt road out near Callahan's. It was the younger Cahill boy out there. They were looking to trade drugs with some people from Melbourne. I interrupted that. We went back to their place. I was in the passenger seat, he was driving. And we hit a kangaroo.'

'In their car?'

'Yes. And he was hurt. So I took care of him and took him back to his dad's.'

'Weren't they mad?'

'They were mad to begin with but I think he'll be fine.'

'The younger one is Sidney?'

'Yeah, that's him. He'll be alright. The roo cut him up a bit, though.'

'And so what happened to your car?'

His toast sprang up and he grabbed it. While he buttered he said, 'So I drove their car back to my car. Plan was to leave it the same way I found it. But when I got back to my car somebody had slashed the tyres.'

'Somebody? Who?'

'I don't know who.'

'Vernie—'

'Don't Vernie me.'

'You know what I heard down the street? That there were some blokes from Melbourne in the pub last night, gave that young policeman Jack a bit of a hiding. I bet it was them, looking for the drugs. Dirty business.'

'Well, even if it was them they don't know it was me took the car.'

'Of course they know it was you. They will have talked to Ernie. Where's their car now?'

'You don't know they talked to Ernie.'

'Where's the car?'

He ate his toast. She could be right about Ernie. The truth of it sat like mustard on his tongue. He said, 'I stashed it down at the river.'

'Where you put the boat in sometimes?'

He nodded.

'How'd you get back here, then?'

'I walked.'

She sighed, and said, 'You're an idiot sometimes.'

This hurt him worse than his pained calves.

Then he said, 'The drugs are in that car.'

'Well, that means they're going to want it!'

He nodded. 'I know.'

'So? We should go and get it and give it back.'

'I'm not sure we should. Let's just see how they react first. Make sure they're leaving Caleb alone.'

'These Melbourne guys came and thought nothing of beating up a policeman. They'd think nothing of . . . and me in the process? Don't you care?'

'Of course I bloody care.'

'Then get the car.'

He sat there impassive. She glared at him, all the resentment in the world on her face. Him just taking it.

Soon, without another word, she stomped from the kitchen and slammed the front door. He put more bread in the toaster. Heard her car start and peel down the driveway. Once, she would have gone to her folks, but they were dead now, been gone two decades. She was probably going to Margie's, the old bag, the gossip. Where she normally ran off to after a fight. He went to Snake Island, she went to her friend's. They'd be talking about him the moment her foot left the car and met Margie's pavement.

~

He was sitting on his chair out the back with a cup of tea, staring at the pelican's grave, when he heard a car pull into the driveway. He creaked up, knees and calves and back aching, and walked through the house to the front door. As his hand went to the doorknob there came a pounding that rattled the wood.

'Vernon Moore? You in there?' a female voice shouted.

He took a moment.

'Yeah?'

'It's Sharon Wornkin. The police.'

'I know who you bloody are,' he said as he opened the door. She stood ready at the bottom of his doorstep. Hands on her hips, eyeing him carefully.

'What do you want?'

'I need to have a word,' she said.

Vernon hated the way she was looking at him. Hated her ill-fitting uniform. It bulged at every button.

'Have it then,' Vernon said.

'We need to take a drive.'

'Why?'

'We need to have a word.'

'You arresting me?'

'I suppose I am.'

Absurd, the way she was looking up at him with her hands on her hips. He breathed slowly out, looked at the clouds on the horizon.

'What for?'

'For stealing.'

'Stealing what?'

'A car. Come on, Vernon, don't make me cuff you.'

Vernon looked down at her. 'You think that gun on your hip there scares me?'

Exasperation on her face now. 'Come on, Vernon. Just get in the car.'

'Alright, alright, let me get my jacket.'

He found his jacket, crumpled in a heap on the floor beside the bed, and shrugged it on. He put his keys in his pocket and went outside, deadlocking the front door. He walked to the cruiser and got in the passenger seat.

Sharon, following, opened the passenger door again. 'What do you think you're doing?'

'I'm in the car, like you asked.'

'Not up there. Get in the back.'

'Why?'

'Prisoners sit in the back.'

'Bloody hell. Get off your high horse a bit.'

She waited for him to lever himself out and get in the back before getting in herself. She started the ignition, backed down the driveway. As she looked out past Vernon's head to the rear of the car he made sure his expression said nothing.

~

At the station, she showed him to a plastic chair for him to sit on. He was reminded of the prison chair in which he'd sat the previous day.

Sharon approached the counter, which looked like a kitchen bench. Sitting behind was a young policeman—judging by his face, the one who'd encountered the Melbourne thugs.

'You okay, Jack?' Sharon asked him, leaning forward awkwardly on the counter.

'That Vernon Moore?'

'I'm right bloody here,' Vernon said. 'Don't need to talk about me like I'm not.'

The injured man looked at him. 'Are you Vernon Moore?'

'I just said that's me.'

The cop turned back to Sharon. 'Is he in trouble?'

'Hand over your things,' she said to Vernon. He grumbled, stood, and handed over the car keys and wallet. The injured bloke put them in a small, white basket, and said, 'He need a room?'

'Yeah.'

'They're all free. Take the end one.'

'Sounds like I'm checking into a resort,' Vernon said, and was ignored.

'Good. Alright,' Sharon said. 'Can you help me get him in there?'

The two of them walked Vernon down a corridor. He couldn't help but feel he was already manacled, a prisoner from a time past. They led him to a cell, iron bars, and sat him down. A strip of bench lined one side entirely and in the corner was a steel toilet. Sharon stood at the entrance while Jack helped him inside.

'I was in the war, you know,' Vernon said, and felt a git for doing so.

'Yeah? Your legs hurt or something?'

'Yeah. They do.'

'Maybe you're just old? Nothing to do with war?'

'You speak to all your elders like that?'

'Can I have your hand, please?'

Vernon offered him a hand, his wrinkled palm upright. Before Vernon could react he was handcuffed to the bench, through a small metal hoop. He shook the metal. Cold against his skin.

'Now, come on, Sharon. There's no need for this.'

Jack looked at his sergeant and received a nod of recognition for his efforts. He left the cell, leaving Vernon alone with Sharon, who stood in the doorway with her arms crossed. Some primal fear of confinement, reminiscent of his army days, surged through him.

'There's no bloody need for the cuffs!'

'Sure there is.'

'You wanted to have a word? Let's have the bloody word. Get these off.' He shook his manacled hand. 'Take them off and we'll talk.'

Sharon did not unfold her arms. 'We'll talk in a bit.'

'What do you mean? Come on. Sharon!'

'I've got some work to do, then I'll be back.'

'You mongrel,' Vernon said as she shut the door. 'Come back! At least undo the cuffs.'

He sat there alone. Sat and stared at nothing at all. He couldn't even put his head in his hands. He rattled the chain, squeezed his wrist with his other hand. Truly a prisoner now. His thoughts turned to the pelican again and its outstretched wing, caked in gunk. Its prison was within it, plastic choking the life from its lungs. Imagine swallowing that whole.

~

The pelican. The image of it. Babes at its breast, open wounds flowing. Their greedy beaks overflowing with the life of their mother. And now, maybe too late, he'd finally given something of himself for his son. Being locked away in here felt noble. And stupid. The pelican's plan sounded like it would work. He barely had a plan. Probably he'd only made things worse.

He sat for what felt an age. His knees ached, but it was too awkward to get his hand there for a rub. He started to call out. Nothing specific, a primal yell, bouncing off everything. He wondered if Jack was still about. He yelled again. Sitting on the bench made his arse cold. He managed to massage it, the old flesh moulding to his fingertips. He was at this task when he heard, footsteps approaching, the door open.

'It's about bloody time, Sharon. I need to piss.'

Instead Vernon saw William Kelly's face. The man wore none of his usual smile, or ease.

'Bill,' Vernon said.

'Hello, Vernon.'

'What're you doing here?'

William did not sit. He stood near the door—was he scared that his old friend had turned feral in imprisonment, would claw his eyes out

Soon there were sounds outside, a person's voice. Her door opened and she was hauled out by her underarms, and shakily she stood and glared at the sun. There was a policeman beside her, looking at her face, her forehead, saying something. Sirens in the distance. The policeman was nodding to the grass—asking her to sit down? She kept running her hands over her belly. Her grief was such that she could not sit.

~

When she woke she instinctively looked for her husband in the empty space beside her. She'd dreamed of Mark again. That he'd been born. That she'd got to hold him. There was a poster on the wall of some woman draped over the front of a car, grinning like some possum snarling in the dark. Wearing knee-high boots. Margie's boy's room. She rolled onto her back and looked at the ceiling. Stains in each corner, the fan dusty. She was too old for this now, fighting like this. It was childish. She sighed and kicked off the doona.

Margie wasn't up yet, often wouldn't rise until eight at least. With her husband dead and her boy moved to Trenton as an electrician, Margie had given up all reason to live besides gossip. And you didn't need to wake up early to catch gossip.

Penelope sat up and swung her feet around. She hadn't brought her slippers, in her rush to leave, and so padded barefoot on the carpet to the bathroom across the hallway. She showered. When she was ready to leave, and had her towel wrapped around her and her hair up in another, she wiped her hand across the mirror and stared at her weathered reflection. Wanted to scold herself, force herself to look at who she'd become, truly. After getting dressed she walked to the kitchen.

She ate a bowl of cornflakes, seated at the meagre, laminex table, the same table William Kelly had sat at yesterday, being polite with his words but judging her with his thoughts, she knew. She thought of her husband and the way he had looked when she left him alone in their house. She looked at the bowl of cereal, the spoon hovering before her lips. She searched the orange flakes for something. He was stuck to her like tar. Without him she was less of herself and she wondered if he felt the same.

Margie soon approached from her bedroom. With her blue dressing gown flowing about her she looked both elegant and whale-like, slow-moving and graceful. Her stomach collided with the kitchen bench and she grimaced, grabbed at it.

'You alright?' Penelope asked.

'I'm okay, I'm okay. Gosh, that hurt,' she said. She opened the fridge, prepared her cornflakes. 'So Phyllis called me this morning with some more news about your man.'

Always the feigned delight when she spoke about another's misfortune, even those she cared for. 'Yeah?' Penelope asked. 'What's that?'

'Well, Phyllis said she was talking to Julia, and you know Julia. She's friends with Ruth. Married to Jack?'

Penelope only nodded. They'd been through this the day before. William Kelly had told them first, but Margie had taken great delight in confirming the information to be true through her own network.

'So,' Margie said, 'Phyllis said that Julia said your old man got released. And Julia said Ruth said Jack is quitting the force! She's so upset, with a baby on the way. Can't blame him really, though. I heard those blokes who beat him up the other night got released with just a warning. No small wonder in this town. Nothing ever gets prosecuted properly. You know I heard Sharon Wornkin say she didn't really care about Newbury? Somebody was trying to tell her about their milk getting retested down at the supermarket—you know how Trenton gets with the milk?—and they'd found some abnormalities, or some other word. And she said she didn't really care. I know the job is hard for her, but I heard her say it. Can you believe that?'

Penelope slowly nodded, trying to pick out the important information.

Margie walked over and sat at the table. 'You don't seem too happy about it.'

'Too happy about what? You said a lot just now, Margie.'

'Vernon's release.'

'Well. I'm glad, I suppose.'

Margie took a mouthful of cereal. 'I understand that. I was the same with Doug—'

Penelope knew she was about to get the story again, so she said quickly, 'I was thinking we could play bowls again today.'

Margie stuttered, clearly wanted to continue on. She soon recovered and said, 'I know it sounds dumb, but I like it when you two fight. I want you to make up with Vernon as soon as possible, don't get me wrong'—she said without an ounce of sincerity—'but I really like having you here. Reminds me of when things were a bit better.'

Penelope stood and moved to the sink. She rinsed out her bowl and when she turned around Margie added, 'Makes me think of your boy. Actually, I meant to say, we should go visit him.'

'We?'

'Well,' Margie said, and looked down at her bowl, 'I mean, only if you want me to come. But I'd be happy to go with you.'

'So you can talk about it with everybody?'

Penelope regretted the words the instant they were spoken. Margie's face sagged, her belly fell forward. She gave a hefty sigh. There was no defiance or defence in her, just acknowledgement. That this was the way it was.

Penelope tried to make amends. 'You're right. I guess we should.'

Margie looked up. 'You've just been talking about it a lot and I thought I could go and support you. Help you.'

'I know.'

'So if you don't want me there I won't be there.'

BEN HOBSON

'No,' Penelope said, 'it was a good idea. I'm sorry. We should go.'

'After lunch?'

'How about later this afternoon. That's visiting hours anyway.'

Margie looked surprised. 'You know when they are?'

Penelope nodded. 'We'll go then.'

When Penelope turned to leave the room, Margie said, 'What are you going to do about Vernon?'

'That man has never needed me for anything. If he starts now he'll know how to find me.'

Getting ready for bowls, she tried to forget what her son had looked like the day before he had hurt that young woman for the final time. The last time Penelope had seen him. The way he had laughed as though everything had been fine.

164

NINETEEN

~

SIDNEY CAHILL

Brendan was out in the shed. Had been most of yesterday, too. Working on something. Sidney could hear his banging from the bathroom. Amy was sitting in the bath splashing happily, looking up at him for reaction, but his thoughts were not with her. The Cahill family had eaten fish for lunch, steamed cod with white sauce, what they always ate on Good Friday, seated in silence around the dining table. Cassie had not re-emerged from her bedroom since Brendan had been beaten, apart from grabbing small amounts of food. His mother sat grim-jawed and hard to read. She spoke once to Brendan, tended him with sympathy, but soon shut up when Ernie rested a hand on her arm, gave her a look. Brendan's face was swollen, faint notes of purple up his neck.

The only normal one among them while they ate had been their father. He had the same jovial manner he always ate with, as though nothing had happened. His were the only words uttered the whole meal, complimenting his wife on her cooking. It was all in stark contrast to their usually loud family. This disturbed Sidney more than anything.

Amy had pasted most of her fish over her face and after lunch her face had broken out in a rash, which she kept scratching. He'd tried moisturiser on it but she had protested to the point of screaming. Sarah had been no help. Even now she was in the bedroom, ignoring her daughter. The bath had calmed Amy down, though. She wasn't watching her father now, focusing instead on the bath toys. He splashed some water at her.

Leaning on the bathtub, he could feel the fractured rib in his chest. He could feel, too, the bristles of the stitches rubbing against the fabric of his shirt. He felt pretty stupid, how badly he'd reacted. He'd thought he was dying. Brendan would've taken the kicks in stride and kept going, tackled the old man. His arm still hurt. He moved into a better position, sitting cross-legged. Sitting forward, Sidney dabbed at Amy's face again with the face washer. With his poor arm, the shoulder ached. She cried and waved her hand at his in protest. The rash still lit up her face but it no longer seemed to be spreading. Maybe she had an allergy? 'Maybe it's just Grandma's cooking, hey sweetheart?' and she offered him a smile.

Mid afternoon, with his daughter washed, dried and asleep, Sidney walked outside. His brother's project in the shed was still underway, judging by the sounds. The pig carcass swinging on the verandah a grim reminder. It wasn't that their father hadn't beaten them before, but there'd always been a reason, and it had always seemed measured. He thought of Amy, of what he'd do were she to become a threat to herself. Would he react the same way? If she were endangering herself, or their family, what lengths would he go to to stop her? Shook his head. Hard to understand or judge that sort of thing until it's on you. The pig's skin was slowly losing its pink. They'd bathed it in boiling water to rid it of its hair, the bath still beside the verandah, around the side of the house.

Sidney walked to the shed. He stuck his head inside. His brother had taken most of the tin drums of petrol, which were used to fuel up in a pinch, and moved them to the other side of the shed. There were still hundreds of pots of marijuana growing at the other end of the shed. The humidifier in the back was pumping air; Brendan looked sweaty.

Sidney stepped into the shed. Brendan, hefting a drum, first smiled at him then grimaced, swallowed and glared, like his true mood had swallowed the false.

'What're you doing?'

'Just organising.'

'You want a hand?'

'No. She's right.'

Sidney paused. 'You know, Dad didn't mean it.'

Brendan shook his head. 'It's not that. I was an arsehole. Wornkin said she got the car back, right?' He started his walk back to the drums.

'Why're you moving the fuel?'

'Needed doing.'

Sidney nodded, knew that wasn't true. Brendan probably just needing to do something physical. How he'd always been. 'She said the car'll be here this afternoon.'

'And all the boxes were still in it?'

'She said so, but she wouldn't know different.'

'Alright then,' Brendan said, hefting another drum. He waddled back across the shed. His shirt was pasted to his back with sweat, the tendons of his arms stretched.

'How's her rash?'

'I think it's alright. It's calming down.'

'That's good.'

'What did you mean you were an arsehole?'

Brendan set the drum down and looked at him. 'That mongrel deserved all he got. Deserved more. But I've never done nothing to cause you or Cass harm. Or Mum and Dad. And that's what I did.'

Sidney nodded. 'That you apologising?'

'I guess it is.'

'So that's why you're in the mood?'

'Well, that, and Dad stuck my head inside a pig and held me there and tried to kill me.'

Sidney laughed, and Brendan joined him. And in the sound of their laughter was the reassurance that the family would soon return to normal. The thought gave Sidney pause. Their normalcy might not be something he wanted. Brendan claimed to be sorry—but how long would that last? Was normal Brendan something either of them wanted?

He watched his brother a moment longer, his great hulking frame, then walked from the shed. He sat inside at the dining table and listened for his little girl's crying, but no crying came.

~

Later that afternoon he heard a car approach. Sharon had been and gone, leaving the Commodore, Cassie driving her back into town. Cassie claimed she was going to visit Peter anyway, but maybe she was still aiming to avoid things. Brendan had checked on the product, satisfied himself it was all there, and their father had clapped him on the back. The two had even shared a smile. They had all been there except for Cassie. Even Sarah had emerged; Amy had been on Sidney's arm. The family's malaise had slowly lifted. Brendan had taken Amy and thrown her in the air and caught her in his arms. She had laughed and laughed and gripped a hold of him as he had counted up to three, on the three launching her, her little legs churning, delight and terror on her face. Sidney had watched, his arm around Sarah.

The car trundled up the driveway and stopped before the house. It wasn't a car that Sidney knew. He was on the verandah with Amy, playing with her dollhouse, trying not to strain his arm. Amy was making the dolls collide with each other, knocking down her father's efforts with unrestrained pleasure. She giggled as she struck his blocks and sent them sprawling, a small dam of colour.

'Brendan!' he shouted now, standing up, his eyes not leaving the car.

'What?' his brother said, from inside.

'You hear the car?'

'Who is it?'

'Don't know.'

Nobody was getting out. Sidney squinted to see who was inside. The driver killed the engine. Then the door opened and out stepped the old man. He was limping.

'You got the gun this time?' Sidney demanded. He looked to his daughter.

'No, mate,' the old man said. 'No gun.'

Sidney looked at him. The old man's face was swollen and he was slumped over. He had been on the receiving end of something bad. He was holding his belly as though he had been gored.

Brendan appeared beside Sidney. 'What do you want?' he said to the old man. Coldness in his voice.

'Just want a chat with Ernie.'

'You bring your gun?'

'Ask your brother.'

Brendan leaned over to Sidney. 'You take Amy inside.'

Sidney scooped up his daughter. As he turned to go he caught the old man's eyes and saw shock.

'Didn't realise you had a little one.'

'Yeah. Well.'

Sidney walked inside. He shuffled down the hallway. Their father was on his bed, his feet up, reading a novel, an alien of some sort on the front. He looked up as his son entered the room.

'Who's outside?'

'The old bloke. Vernon?'

His father instantly stood. He strode down the hallway and only said, 'You give that girl to her mother.'

Sidney followed. He entered his room and saw his wife on their bed, staring at the ceiling. Either deep in thought or completely out of it.

'You need to take Amy.'

'Why?'

'You just do, alright? Here.'

He placed his daughter on the bed. Sarah remained lying down, his daughter clambering over her as he shut the door.

There were voices in the kitchen. He heard the kettle being boiled. He went in and found the three of them already around the table.

The old man looked up at Sidney and smiled sadly. 'Count the days with her, mate. Like that'—he clicked his fingers—'and they'll be grown up and arguing with you.'

Sidney did not know what to say to this. He sat down next to his father, who said, 'So what do you want, Moore?'

The old man sighed. 'Suppose you know why I'm looking like this.'

Ernie said nothing, had his arms crossed.

'Anyway. I came up here to call a truce. I want to apologise for taking the car, for taking your son by gun point. I was wrong.'

'Bloody right you were,' Brendan said, not looking at Vernon. Ernie's face betrayed nothing.

The old man paused a moment. 'That's what I said. I know I did wrong.'

'Right,' Brendan said. With the kettle boiled he put some tea bags into some cups and poured in the water. Nobody spoke. Brendan busied himself, maybe in an effort to avoid doing with his hands what he truly wanted. Soon he approached them all with steaming cups, the old man included. He sat down next to Sidney, still without looking up.

'So I want to apologise for all of it,' the old man continued. 'I hope you can understand'—his eyes took in Ernie's—'that I was a father doing something desperate, and nothing more. Never meant any harm for your boy here. How's the arm, mate?'

Sidney shrugged. 'It was just dislocated.'

Ernie said, after a moment, 'Is that it?'

'Well,' the old man said, shifting in his chair, sipping at his tea. 'I was hoping to just chat and sort it all out.'

'Sort what all out?'

'My boy. Leaving my boy alone. Me leaving you lot alone.' Ernie said nothing to this. Finally he added, 'Come on, mate. Already feel like a git doing this.'

'I already told you I'd tell my boy to leave off yours.'

'You know what I want, mate. I want your guarantee.'

'You're not in a position to bargain.'

The old man breathed out slowly. 'I know I'm not. I'm not trying to bargain.'

'I've known blokes like you my whole life, Moore. Wondered why I didn't recognise you. It's because you think you're not a part of this town. You don't get involved, don't talk to people. You think you're better than the rest of us. When I was at school there was a bloke like you in my year, thought he was better than everybody else because he was better at everything. Better at school, at footy, at everything. At getting with women. Stole my missus. Thought he could, anyway. Just entitled to it. Really thought the lay of the land was I'd just roll over, accept it. Just the way he thought it was, how the universe worked. Taught him he was wrong with the band end of a broken beer glass. Still can't look straight, last I heard.'

Silence immediately following this. Ernie sipped at his tea.

'Bloody hell,' the old man finally said. His hands splayed out on the table. His eyes took in their ceiling. 'I was trying to come up here and talk to you. Not get all huffy about it.'

'Point is people can think they're above the rest of us all they like, they'll still get hurt the same. You think you're entitled to something here? You're not.'

The old man's eyes tightened. 'I came up to give you my apology and I've done that. Didn't ask for a speech. Didn't need one.' He sat back, crossed his arms. 'All I want is your guarantee. That's it. I think that's bloody reasonable.'

'I don't guarantee anything.'

'So I guess that's all I'm getting then,' he said. 'Suppose I should leave.'

His father said nothing for a moment. Sidney looked at all the silent men, unfolded his arms and said, 'At least finish your tea.'

'I think I'll go.'

He stood. Sidney and Ernie both remained seated but, to Sidney's surprise, Brendan stood. 'I'll see you out.'

The old man took a moment, surveying the room, then nodded.

'I don't think I'm better than people.'

'You act like it, but,' Ernie said.

The old man paused, then nodded again and turned, hunched over, limping. Brendan even held the door open for him.

After they'd exited, his father turned to Sidney and said, 'Some nerve, hey.'

'He was just trying to apologise, Dad.'

Ernie shook his head, leaned back on his chair. 'He was trying to manipulate us into getting his way.'

'You just said the other night you'd do anything for us. He's just doing that, isn't he?'

Ernie nodded slowly, breathed out. 'Yeah, I guess.' His shoulders slumped a bit. He leaned forward, the chair resting, and took some tea. 'How's the rash on your little one?'

'I think it's clearing up.'

'Good,' his father said. 'You moisturise her skin?'

'You know about this?'

His father laughed a little. 'I used to put you on my arm, like this,' he said, and positioned his arm horizontal to the table, indicated the length of his forearm. 'You used to fit right here.'

'You say that a lot.'

'Do I?'

'Yeah.'

'Well. I used to put that moisturiser all up and down your back. You used to get a bad rash on your back when you slept at night. On your butt.'

Brendan re-entered the house. He walked to the table and slouched into a chair. Ernie's arm lowered.

'You didn't kill him, did you?' he asked.

'No. He's alright.'

'You didn't say anything else to him?'

Brendan shook his head.

'I want this done with. It's finished now. You understand me?'

Brendan nodded. 'I get it.'

They sat around the table drinking their tea. Sidney watched his brother and his father and tried to see something of his daughter in them but couldn't. She was wholly unique and a part of him. These men were not. The thought arrived with no sadness. Just a deep under-standing of something he had known since Amy was born.

TWENTY

~

VERNON MOORE

It was hard to tell how his apology had been taken, with Ernie as gruff and unreadable as he had been the first time Vernon had been here. And he had some bite to him. Summed up Vernon pretty well. It was unnerving, really. In the end Vernon knew he'd done all he could to right the situation, and as he left their front verandah he hoped it was for the last time.

There was a magpie sitting atop a fence post near his car. Vernon walked, with Brendan keeping pace. He was not afraid of Brendan, strangely. The big lug was mostly talk and hot air. But the bird gave him pause. As he opened his car door he watched it gaze at him as though it knew him.

As Vernon climbed into his car Brendan stepped so close to him he was no longer able to shut the door. Brendan looked down at him, one arm resting on the doorframe. There was a bruising around the edges of his eyes, on his throat, that Vernon had not before noticed. A sneer in his eyes. This man who had beaten his son.

'You get what you wanted?' he asked.

'I know,' she said. She sighed audibly. 'No use you running off without something in your stomach. Come on.'

He shut the front door and walked back inside. 'Maybe some of that ham?'

'I told you, I didn't get the ham.'

'No, the regular ham.'

'A sandwich?'

He seated himself on a stool at the counter, watching his wife move about the kitchen. 'You could toast it,' he said.

'Fusspot.'

'Yeah.'

'You know, you look terrible.'

He rubbed his face, the makings of his grey and meagre beard. The cut on his face sore to the touch. 'I don't feel too good either.'

'Ever since I met you, you've only liked about three different meals.'

He snorted. 'That's not true.'

She raised a hand and counted on her fingers. 'Steak and mash and veg. Ham sandwiches, toasted. Sausages and mash and veg.'

He shook his head. 'I like more than that.'

'Beer?'

'Yeah. Beer.'

She sighed. 'That's not a meal. You're an old fool.'

'I know.'

'You're my old fool, though.'

He returned her smile. 'Yes. I am.'

~

The darkness surrounding Penelope's car seemed thicker than usual. Maybe because of the street he was in. He was parked near the bridge running into Newbury, around twenty minutes from Port Napier, on the way to the Cahills'. He'd pulled off the road next to the bridge and driven down a slope to the side and parked his car and turned off the lights. It took him a while to solidify his plan. He sat staring at the bridge, the rusted hulk of it, and thought on the possibilities. No good options, just drastic ones.

He left the car, shutting the door quietly. He opened the back door and lifted his axe from the seat, the weight of it hurting his fingers. The police station was on Bedford Road, not five hundred metres from where he stood. He ambled up to the road and stared down it, trying to make out the shape of the station in the distance, and if there were any police cars out front, but for all the streetlamps he couldn't see anything. He rubbed his old eyes, squinted, and kept walking.

The building he was aiming for was on his right. It was lit dimly by one bulb behind a plastic casing over the front door. He crept up, the dull sound of whirring machinery within. There was nobody about. The axe head, in the dull light, showed the dried pelican blood. He hadn't cleaned it well at all. He wondered if there was an alarm, but had no idea how to check for such a thing. There was a Neighbourhood Watch sign in the front window, the white people shapes against the diamond green, but there was no indication, anywhere, of anybody watching.

Vernon swung the axe lightly against the door handle, blade up, but the handle did not break. He looked around, lifted the axe once more and dropped it down, putting his aching shoulder into it. The handle sprung free and clattered to the concrete, loud in the dark. He shouldered into the door before he could doubt himself and tensed for an alarm to sound. He waited. Nothing.

He walked through this building he had never been in before. There were plastic strips dangling over certain doorways, air conditioning pumping throughout. He entered a room and saw the barrels he wanted near the doorway. Big bastards. He put the axe down on the floor and got his shoulder into one, trying to lift it. It was heavier than he'd expected. There was liquid inside, sloshing about, and as he lifted, it hit one of the sides and the weight sent the barrel toppling to the ground. He braced for the impact, the sound of it, but the plastic barrel on the linoleum floor was almost silent.

With a lot of effort he managed to get two barrels to the front door—a combination of carrying, kicking and rolling, the barrels constantly banging into the walls, every part of him sore and aching. He was breathing hard and sweating by the time he made it outside. He stood with his hands on his hips and let the breeze cool him. A car motored down Bedford Road, its lights traversing the bitumen. He looked down at the barrels, estimated the travel time to his car.

Leaving them where they were he walked back to the bridge, down the slope to the car. Gunning the engine, the old thing struggling back up the slope. Throwing his earlier precaution aside, he backed up to the front door of the building and popped the boot. He was soon driving with the two barrels of liquid secured within, the axe next to the shotgun across the back seat.

~

As he drew closer to the farmhouse he started to curse his lack of forethought. He slowed the car to a crawl and stopped in the dirt at the side of the road. None of the lights were on at the farm, not even in the shed. There were clouds overhead. He stepped out of the car and sat on the bonnet and put his arms around himself. His ribs ached dully. He hadn't brought a jacket, either. He swore and looked back at the house. No way to approach quietly in the car. They'd be sure to hear and stop him before he started. And no way to lug the barrels up by hand, old as he was.

He walked up as quietly as he could, moonlight streaming through the branches overhead. He came to the entry to the property—a sad letterbox atop a fence post, long stretches of barbed-wire fence on either side, the cattle grid beneath his feet. He trod over it carefully, so as not to wedge a foot between the gaps. Then the crunch of gravel. He looked up. Still no lights, no sign of movement, no noise beyond the trees rustling in the breeze and the blood pumping through his ears. He walked off the driveway and onto the grass.

He approached the shed, keeping a wary eye on the house all the while. He rounded the back and found what he was looking for leaning up against the wall: an old wheelbarrow, darkened patches in the night indicating rust. Wooden handles. He lifted it onto its wheel and started pushing, and stopped immediately: the loud squeaking threatened to wake the entire family. His eyes froze on the house. He imagined the light coming on and out of the darkness stepping Ernie, or Brendan, armed with something, aimed at his head, he the pelican lamely flapping its wing. He breathed. Nothing happened.

Vernon stood staring at the wheelbarrow. Then he ventured around the front of the giant shed. The front door was ajar, so he stuck his head in. There on seven long tables were potted plants, standing straight and tall, their leaves dripping moisture in the darkness. An air-humidifier unit was humming somewhere. A wonder the Cahills didn't shut the front door, keep the air in. Large, flat, hydroponic lights were suspended from the roof. He walked inside, careful not to knock the door upon entry. The plants swayed slightly, as though acclimating to his presence. He reached out a hand to feel the leaves of one.

He noticed a cupboard against a wall and opened it, turning the handle as quietly as possible. The door creaked a little as he pulled it. Plenty of tools in here. A can of old motor oil near the bottom. He took this and didn't bother shutting the door.

He coated the axle of the wheelbarrow, and the dense blackness of the oil seemed to swallow the moonlight. He squinted to see better, felt the slime coating his fingertips. When he was done he flipped the wheelbarrow back onto its wheel and hesitantly pushed it forward. There was still a squeaking, although it was mostly muffled. He would risk it.

He wheeled the barrow on the grass and thought about what he could do. What choices he had. He had to bloody fix things. Fill the lack he'd left in his family. There were no good ways through, far as he could tell. All that was left was this.

With a great struggle he manoeuvred the barrels into the wheelbarrow. Fortunately both fit at once. Before making the trek back he got into the car and sat for a moment. He opened the glove compartment and took the lighter he had brought and put it in the pocket of his pants. He got out of the car and started his return journey.

By the time he had reached the shed his back was aching. His knees felt as though they would seize up. He rested the barrow and sat down and rubbed at his knees, his shins. He had never felt so old. Light was beginning to peek up over the horizon.

He opened the shed door wide and wheeled in his load. Carefully, with a straining back, he lifted both barrels out and put them on the floor. The car he'd returned earlier that day parked near a couch. Useless bloody gesture. In the cupboard he found a Phillips head screwdriver, which he stabbed into the base of a barrel. The plastic gave quickly and the liquid spilled out, covering his hands. The chemical smell instantly made him dizzy. He struggled to stand.

Then he stabbed the second barrel. It too started to leak over his hands, his shoes. Tried his damnedest to not make a sound. He fumbled with the lighter, found a flame, and held it to the liquid.

His arm immediately caught fire. He swore loudly and jumped, and, strangely, tried to hug the arm to his chest. As soon as the flame touched the fabric covering his torso he changed his mind and ripped at the shirt, his fingertips searing. He managed to undo the shirt and somehow run without conscious thought out of the shed, into the early morning. The flames inside licked up the spill he'd created. He ripped the shirt off and scrunched the shirt up into a ball, muffling the flames, and pounded at his hands. His eyes went up when he heard the muffled sound of an explosion.

It shook him and threw him down. He landed with a thud on his arse and then fell onto his now naked back in the cold grass. He scrambled up. The door of the house was opening, somebody was rushing out. He tried to run. The flames behind him searing. He jogged as far as his old wounded knees would take him. A magpie, possibly the same he had seen yesterday, squawked at him from its fence post.

TWENTY-FOUR

~

SIDNEY CAHILL

They had both woken when his daughter started to cry. It was a pitiful sound, mournful, full of doubt and fear. He went to her quickly and scooped her up, holding her to his ear. He shushed her as he brought her to her mother: there was only one thing that would soothe her and it wasn't his voice. Sarah, still bleary, sat upright and held Amy to her breast. Soon his daughter was contentedly feasting. He watched. He knew Sarah did not regard this act with the same reverence he held for it. She did not begrudge her daughter but to her she was a cow, a service beast for the suckling. For Sidney this was far more than machinery and mechanism. This was magic. Although there were problems between them, there was also happiness and through this act he knew all three of them would forever be lashed to one another.

He heard a man swear loudly outside.

'What was that?' Sarah asked, her eyes half lidded.

'I don't know.'

He got up from the bed and lifted the curtain and there on the grass was the old man, Moore, running, smoking, shirtless. Running from their shed. Orange flame licking the inside, smoke like blood oozing out of an artery escaping at the corners of the door. Heavy, black. Sidney moaned. He didn't bother with a shirt, he ran out into the hallway half naked, banged on his brother's door then ran to his parents'. He barged through it and his dad was up in a flash, eyes bright and ready.

'What is it?' he asked.

The explosion rocked the house. Sidney gripped the door. His dad was already moving.

'The shed,' Sidney said, running again.

Outside he beheld the building in the midst of its destruction. There were flames on the roof now. No telling how long it had been on fire; when Moore had started it. A red glow coated the sky. He stepped forwards, felt the presence of his brother and his father at his back.

His father swore. 'How much was in there?' he asked, and turned to Brendan, who was already running to the garden hose.

'All that new crop.' Brendan fumbled with the tap until their father shouldered him out of the way.

'Give me that,' he said, and tore the hose from Brendan's hand.

Ernie cranked it on and ran towards the blaze, the meagre stream a cruel joke next to the colour.

'Did you see what happened?' Brendan asked Sidney.

'No.'

'You think it just went up? Light sparked or something?'

'Maybe.'

Their father now turned to his boys and shouted, 'Don't just stand there bloody daydreaming! Get a wheelbarrow and fill it with dirt!'

'Why?'

'To smother the thing!'

Brendan hurried off but Sidney continued to watch as another small explosion sent a burst of orange out of the shed. It engulfed his father, who was inside this monstrous gout of flame for a moment, and then Sidney saw him with fire coating his arms and his face and he was rolling on the ground, screaming in agony, a scream such as Sidney had never heard before, that ripped at something in his chest. He rushed to his father's side.

The hose lay in the grass, still flowing, so Sidney scooped it up and directed the stream at his father, the shed beside him searing his face, his arms. The flames on his father were dying out but the scream, the screaming. It hurt Sidney's ears and was heart-rending, like a pig being gutted. Then Brendan was beside him and Sidney was afraid to look at what damage had been done to his father, this man who had always seemed immune to injury, now so unceremoniously torn down. There was the smell of cooking carcass, of pig on a spit. The smell of burned hair.

The women were all crowded outside the house, standing on the verandah watching the flames, their faces licking gold. Sidney turned to them, the hose still trained, and yelled, 'Call Wilkie!'

'Is he alright?' Sarah yelled. Cassie went inside, presumably to the phone.

'He's been burned!'

Ernie started coughing and leaned to the side and spewed something brown—it dangled from his mouth, all teeth. Sidney knew to keep a steady stream of water over a burn and so he held the spray. His father had stopped screaming now and was groaning.

'What should we do?' Brendan asked, his voice quiet. 'Should we try to move him?'

'I don't know.'

Cassie came running from the verandah, shouting,

'Wilkie said to keep the hose trained on him and that he's on his way.'

His mother, who had been standing motionless with her arms folded around her middle, seemed to take this as a cue to also approach. Sarah went back inside, no doubt to their daughter. The fire was still roaring beside them, a constant heat against his side. The sound of things popping within. Was the car still in there?

His mother and sister were crying, looking down at this once pow-erful man, who in his agony had become a mewling infant.

'How did this happen?' Cassie asked, sniffing.

Brendan kneeled beside their father. He looked as though he wanted to reach out and comfort the old man but feared ripping his oozing skin. 'I don't know.'

Their mother's silent tears coated her cheeks and the firelight danced upon them and made her seem a clown. She didn't say a word, only stood and watched her husband helplessly, like all of them. Sidney kept the hose trained and thought of his daughter.

Wilkie arrived after what felt an age and knelt beside the now-shiv-ering Ernie. He had chucked a few more times and the ground around his head was sodden with bile. The fire had not spread further. Sidney could hear the wailing of sirens in the distance.

'You can lay off the hose now,' Wilkie said.

Sidney threw it down and it snaked in the grass. 'Will he be alright?'

'We need to get him to the hospital,' Wilkie said, standing up. 'I need to call an ambulance.'

~

His father was loaded into the back of the ambulance, a green plastic sheet draped over him. The sun by now had well and truly risen, giving light to all the horrors of his form. Before he'd been covered, Sidney had seen his burnt flesh. Exposed bone, blackened pieces of skin like overcooked roast. Dangling, dripping. Seeping blood congealed against the plastic sheet, great blotches of red, a butcher's apron. They'd shot him full of painkillers but he was still moaning, his eyes closed. Even the oxygen mask seemed to pain him. Brendan walked beside him as they wheeled him away, reaching out his hand in an effort to hold his father's. But he didn't touch him.

When the two paramedics hoisted him into the ambulance, Cassie and his mother climbed in after him. Their father did not look at them as the door was shut.

The firemen had nearly stopped the fire completely. They'd had to run a pump down to the waterhole and gush the muddy water over the shed, which had slowly diminished the blaze. The smoke from it still billowed into the sky and the firemen continued their stream, a few of them surrounding the pyre. Sidney only watched, his arms folded.

It was hard to tell what all this would mean for them. Sidney didn't know whether he should mention seeing the old man Moore or not. It would probably only lead to more grief. Maybe now it was done.

Brendan called out, shattering his thoughts. 'It was that old bastard!'

So he'd figured it. 'Bloody hell,' Sidney said. He ran back to the verandah, where his brother was storming out with a shotgun in his hands.

'Wait, just wait, Brendan! You don't know that.' He grappled with him but was immediately thrown to the wooden floorboards, his sewn-together chest aching.

'Of course it was bloody him! Look!'

Brendan in his fists held the old man's shirt. Blackened, wrecked. 'Who else would it be?'

His daughter crying inside. Brendan kept right on walking, bunching the shirt, and rounded the corner of the house. Sidney heard Brendan's car starting up. The tyres kicked up gravel as Brendan tore down the driveway but before he reached the end another car was there, blocking his exit. The Melbourne car, Sidney saw.

Brendan did nothing for a moment, both cars staring each other down. Then he reversed, too quickly. He turned the car around before he collided with the house. He opened his door and slammed it shut and stood there, arms folded, waiting for Melbourne to come up the driveway.

Sidney strained to see through the Melbourne car's tinted windows.

When the car parked behind Brendan's both doors opened at the same time but no one got out for a moment. Brendan seemed slighted by this and stamped his foot down. Then Martin and Judah appeared, the latter's moustache like smeared-on paint. Martin cast a hand over his eyes like a visor and stared up at the verandah, ignoring Brendan completely. His attention then turned to the charred remains of the shed, still surrounded by firemen. Finally, smiling, he nodded at Brendan.

'Your face looks a bit rough there, mate.'

Brendan glared at him.

'So,' Martin said to Sidney, who was on the verandah, 'how's the arm?'

Sidney had forgotten it hurt. At this mention he noticed the dull throb in the shoulder.

'It's alright.'

Brendan said sharply, 'You need something?'

Martin spread his arms. 'What sort of welcome is that?'

Judah snorted, scuffed his feet in the gravel. 'You got something to drink in there? What's your name again?'

'Sidney.'

'Make us some tea?'

Brendan, his voice quieter, sterner, said, 'I asked you if you wanted something.'

Martin walked towards him and Brendan stepped back, but Martin only sat on the bonnet of Brendan's car and stared at the smouldering remains of the shed, studying the firemen.

'Can I get that tea now?' Judah asked Sidney.

'Any of you know how to do anything right?' Martin said. He pointed at the shed. 'That where you stored the plants?'

'You don't know that,' Sidney said quickly.

Martin, without turning, held up a hand. 'I can take a good guess, though. One of you smoking in there near some bloody petrol fumes or something? Country hicks, eh.'

Neither brother said anything.

'How much of our product—the stuff we've *paid* you for—was in that shed?' Martin looked at Judah and gave him a slight nod. The big man grinned, advanced on Sidney.

'What're you doing?' Sidney said, back-pedalling.

'Getting what we're owed.'

'Stop. Stop!' Brendan said. 'It wasn't us started the fire.'

Judah stopped but kept grinning. Sidney looked at Brendan and in his heart knew what his brother would do. There was nothing Sidney could do to push him off his course and he knew, also, that this road led to their ruin. He saw it all before them. Bloodshed, either theirs or Moore's. That old man with the shotgun across his lap, looking out for his son. His daughter's crying, though it had stopped now, drifted through his mind like some ghostly premonition of tragedy to come.

Brendan said, 'It was Moore. You look in that car you'll see his shirt. He stole the car, probably intends on selling the product. The old bastard lit it up, trying to intimidate us.'

Martin sighed. 'Ah. So Wornkin had it right. Still *your* fault though, isn't it? You think anybody would try something like this in Melbourne?' Martin looked at the sky and sighed dramatically, lurching his shoulders forward, lowering his head. Sidney stole a quick glance at the remains of the shed, hoping the car the old man had returned—or what was left of it—wasn't easily noticeable. Martin got off the bonnet of Brendan's car and turned from them. He unzipped. Soon a steady stream of piss splashed over Brendan's car. The number plate seemed to be his main target. Martin wiggling his hips like he was at a urinal. Surprising he wasn't whistling. Urine pooled near a tyre, bubbling. Brendan clenched his fists, but didn't move otherwise.

He rezipped, turned back to them. Took a moment to compose himself. 'Clearly, we need to teach you how to run this place. Moore needs to be the example you set for the rest of this town. Let him be a testimony about what happens when you cross the Cahills.'

'I've been telling Dad . . .' Brendan said, but instead of finishing this thought he looked at his brother.

'Telling him what?'

Brendan shook his head. 'Never mind.'

Martin sighed again, looked at Judah. 'Are we coming in and helping you fix all this? Or are we having a different conversation?'

Sidney didn't move for a moment, kept his arms crossed. He did not want to invite these two men into the home wherein his wife and daughter rested. The two of them stared at him, Martin tapping one foot, smiling, like he owned the world. The urine still dripping from Brendan's number plate. Sidney knew he had no other option and so said, 'Yeah. Brendan?'

'Yeah. Alright,' he said. He trod up the stairs, the two men following. As he passed by Sidney, Judah reached out a hand and tousled his hair. Sidney stepped back, which made Judah laugh. 'Easy there, mate. Just being friendly.'

He shook his head and beneath his breath, muttered, 'Brendan.' He looked up at the blueness of the day. He took a breath and walked inside.

TWENTY-FIVE

~

VERNON MOORE

William Kelly's study light was on. It was early morning still, the sun just risen. Vernon sat in the car and debated getting out. His naked torso was shivering and hot at the same time. He worried that some of the flesh on his back had melted into the fabric of the seat and would stick there if he moved. And he'd leave the car and see his skin, a red cloud embedded in the fabric.

He leaned forwards and his skin pulled a bit but did not stick. He got out and the cool breeze struck his torso and he hurried over to the window, holding his arms around himself. Trying not to wake Kelly's wife, Francine. The swing Kelly had built his kids an age ago still hung from the tree out front and swayed as if in sympathy as Vernon passed it.

He came to the window and, dancing from foot to foot to ward off the cold, knocked on the glass. A shuffling sound from inside. Soon the curtains were drawn back and Bill Kelly's confused face appeared. He opened the window.

'Vernon, what are you doing here at this hour? Where's your shirt?'

TWENTY-EIGHT

~

CALEB MOORE

He made it to his parents' house. Found the key in the shed, up on the shelf out of sight. He went back and opened the front door and walked inside calling out for them, but nobody answered. He made himself some sandwiches and sat there eating happily, enjoying the ability to make decisions for himself, choose what to do. He was free, though he knew that each moment he spent outside prison meant a longer time in it. It may be worth it, though, if those Cahills were coming for his parents. If he could protect them.

He finished his lunch and went outside and sat in his father's old chair. Memories of his old man reading the newspaper in this chair after a long day at work. Drinking his tea. Caleb playing footy in the backyard, trying not to punt the ball into the water.

He looked at the old shed, got up and walked over. He rounded the corner of the shed and behind it found his father's boat missing. The trailer, too, was gone. He walked back inside and looked around the house. He checked in the garage on the shelf and found their old tent missing. He sat again in the chair outside and looked out at Snake

Island. He knew they'd gone there. Knew it like he knew how to pull his pants up. He must have just missed them.

Leaning up against the back of the shed he found his father's crappy old tinny. The hull rusty. The old man had sold the motor years ago but in Caleb's memory he still used the boat sometimes for fun, putting it in down the embankment when the tide was in, just rowing around. Probably hoping to take his grandkids out in it one day. Some hope of that now. Caleb studied it and saw the oars and moved his bandaged forearm, flapping it like a wounded bird.

He hefted the tinny—tricky with his forearm in its cast—onto its base and shoved it on the grass over to the wall overlooking the water. He shoved it in. It landed with a thunk and immediately was pressed down into the mud beneath the boat. Caleb climbed down the wall and walked over to it, the mud caking his prison-issue boots, the water up his shins. He pushed the boat until it was free of muck and floating and then jumped in himself. He sat up, regarding his old house. He grabbed an oar and started rowing.

He started with his good arm and then tried once with his sore but found the forearm incapable of much force. So he kept on with the good arm, switching from side to side, until it was too fatigued to continue. The sun beat down and he knew he was getting burned, which made everything worse. Sweat soon stained all his clothes. He put his free hand over the side into the salty brine and splashed it over his head, wetting his hair. He kept rowing. Snake Island grew closer to him but it was slow going and by the end of the day he had barely made it over half the distance. He could still see his old home.

The tide was now up and he could not get out if he wanted to and so he laid down in the boat and studied the stars as they formed above him, resting his tired body. He wondered what his parents were doing. He had to get to them. Be with them. He soon somehow managed to fall asleep.

TWENTY-NINE

~

BRENDAN CAHILL

After the visit with Sharon he sat with Martin and Judah in the bakery down the main street, eating pies for lunch. The festival was now over, the street reopened. Streamers and confetti pooling in gutters. The other two taking their time, laughing it up. It pissed Brendan off that they felt no urgency. These two thought they knew it all and had seen it all, and that the people around them were country bumpkins who wouldn't get one over on them.

He knew Mel had always liked this bakery. Knew more about her than he cared to admit. He'd always been interested in her at high school, had even taken to smelling things she'd handled. Nothing creepy, at least he didn't think so. Just things like paper she'd pass him, a bottle of water. His friends all knew, and never said a word to his face about his strange obsession, but he knew they saw weakness in him. When he was around her his brain would piss-fart and moan about and he'd end up a stammering idiot. She took all his hesitation and twittering with good grace.

And the difference in her face now—it made his tendons tighten.

Made him relish the memory of snapping Caleb Moore's forearm. That rotten mongrel. What he'd done to her. Scarred. Her twisted nose. Wished he'd put his foot in the small of that bastard's back and snapped his spine.

The two jokers finally finished their meal and got up. Out in the car they both sat in the backseat, leaving him up the front like a bloody chauffeur. He felt a right dickhead driving these two around like that and he sank low in his seat, hoping no one would see him.

'Look at them,' Martin said. 'Look at them.'

'Who?' Brendan said.

'Your people, mate. The people in this town. Just take a look at them.'

'What about them?'

Brendan did look. The people were just people. Back to normal after the festival. One fat slob walking across the street with his gut wobbling like a hippo glanced up at the car as it bore down on him and smacked it angrily as it passed. He was wearing a blue flannel shirt tucked into jeans. Old Frank Forster. Brendan knew him from the hardware store. Reinforced the station's door, apparently. Old Frank Forster who whenever you went in wouldn't stop complaining about his back starting to seize up when he worked not working so much nowadays.

He kept driving the car Martin had pissed on. Out of the town and past farmland with cows munching grass or lying down in the shade of trees. Through his mind flashed the pain etched in Sharon's face. He kept going, took the left that led down to Port Napier.

'Where does this guy live?' Judah asked.

'I don't know.'

'What do you mean you don't know?'

'I mean, I thought we'd just look for it.'

Judah snorted. 'You're a git.'

Brendan said nothing to this. Knew he could just ask and find the house almost instantly. He passed the cemetery on the right, drove down the long stretch of road cloaked in green on either side, and came to the roundabout. Ahead was the main part of Port Napier, where the fish and chip shop was. There wasn't much to the town. He turned left, into the small housing estate.

'He'll live here somewhere,' Brendan said. 'Just look out for his car.'

'Isn't his car out bush? With its tyres slashed?' Judah asked.

Brendan kept driving, pretending like he'd remembered that.

Martin leaned forward and said, 'You'd forgotten. Right? It's alright. Listen. I get it. Your dad does the thinking for you. Nothing wrong with that. Like Judah here. Better as a heavy hitter. World needs all sorts. But if you're driving us around on the back of a prayer, well, just admit it.'

Brendan gripped the wheel, making the rubber squeak. 'We just need to ask somebody and they'll tell us.'

As he said this he saw an old man watering his front garden. Slowing the car he wound down his window and shouted, 'Hey, can you tell me where Vernon Moore lives?'

The old man squinted into the sun and said, 'Hello to you, too.'

'Hi. Sorry.'

'It's alright. Manners always a good way to start off a conversation though.'

Brendan did his best not to open his door and choke the mongrel. Instead he said, 'I'm sorry, I said.'

'Now who's asking about Vernon?'

'Just a friend.'

'What sort of friend?'

'I'm a friend of his son's.'

The old man gave him a harsh look. 'Up to no good, that one.'

'Can you just tell me, please?'

'You're not up to no good, are you?'

'No, sir. Just wanting to see how he's doing. With Caleb in jail. Thought he might need somebody to talk to.'

The old man did not seem appeased, but said, 'Oh, alright. Turn right down the next street and he's at the end, just on the water.'

When Brendan rounded the corner he saw a police cruiser at the end of the street. It was parked outside the last house before the water, what Brendan assumed was Vernon Moore's home. Next to it was a mustard-coloured car. He pulled in to the kerb and turned around to face the men in the back.

'What is it?' Martin asked.

'You don't see the cops?'

'Oh, them,' he said. He squinted, leaning forwards. 'Do they matter?'

'Looks like Trenton cops.'

'Okay, but do they matter?'

Brendan said, 'They don't not matter.'

'Come on,' Martin said. 'Just pull into the driveway like you own the place.' He sat back.

'They'll ask questions.'

'So pretend you're his son. It won't be a problem.'

Judah said, 'Just do it, you pansy.'

Brendan, furious, thrust the gearstick into first and revved the car. He pulled into the driveway and, without looking back at his passengers, stepped out.

The doors of the police car were opening. Brendan, with acute fear, went over to the two officers.

'Hey there,' he said, and felt an idiot.

'You live here?' the first policeman asked. They were both young. The second one, standing a metre behind and trying to act tough, had pimples covering his chin.

'My dad lives here,' Brendan said.

'Oh yeah? You know where he is?'

'He's not home?'

'He didn't answer when we knocked.'

Brendan pretended to think on this. 'Guess he's out then.'

'You know where?'

'He hangs out at the pub sometimes.'

'In Newbury?'

'No. Darlington.'

'Where's Darlington?'

'You would've driven through it on your way here.'

'The place with one milk bar and a pub?'

'Yeah. Just past the cemetery, going from Newbury to out here.'

'That's a town?'

'That's Darlington.'

Both policemen laughed. The first said, 'Guess that's all you need.'

Brendan tried to smile. 'If he's not home I'll try him there, then.'

'Alright. Cheers, mate. Hey,' the officer said, and put his hand on Brendan's shoulder to stop him turning. 'You know what's happening with him?'

'No.' Brendan said.

'You know Wornkin?'

Brendan nodded, remembered her face as Judah struck her with his boots. 'The police sergeant.'

'She was being cagey about the whole thing, didn't tell us much,' the officer said. He added, 'We just got word, too, over the radio that Caleb— your brother?—escaped from Boodyarn a few hours ago. The car he took is that one just there'—he nodded—'so he's probably taken the old man's car and bolted. Anyway. Just maybe watch out for your dad. He might be in trouble. We might go look for him at that pub ourselves, actually.'

'I'll leave you to it, then.'

'You should tag along, mate. Help him see a friendly face.'

Brendan looked back at the car. 'I only came to see him quick. I'm in a bit of a hurry.'

'Yeah? Where to?'

'A party. Got my mates in the car.'

He nodded at the car. Martin, for his part, raised a hand, smiling.

'Alright,' the officer said. 'You don't know where Caleb is, do you? You haven't seen him?'

'We don't exactly get along. If he's out he won't come see me.'

'Alright. If you say so. Contact the police, obviously, if you see him or hear anything, okay? We'll go check out Darlington. Not sure what we'll do if we can't find him.'

Brendan nodded. 'Thanks for the work, officer.'

He walked back to the car, looking at the windows at the front of the house, hoping to catch sight of a hand, a face, any movement behind the curtains. But he saw nothing.

He climbed in.

Martin said, 'Well?'

'Well, he's not home, at least.'

'You're sure?'

'The cops're sure.'

Martin said. 'Guess we'll go see his son.'

'Can't do that, either. Caleb's run off.'

'Run off?'

'Boodyarn's minimum security,' Brendan said. 'So he's piss-bolted.'

Martin sat back. Ran his hands over his face. 'Guess that leaves William Kelly from the visitor's log.'

'Bit of a longshot.'

'What other shot do we have?'

~

Before they visited Reverend Kelly, Brendan begged a moment from Martin and Judah to check in with his sister at the hospital about his dad and, after dropping them off at the pub, had found the doctors were now confident his father would pull through. This idea comforted him—he loved his father with a devotion known by few—but it also stabbed at the base of his neck. He knew the burning of his father's skin had been his fault entirely. Nobody else's. His father had told him to lay off and he hadn't. That mongrel Moore getting under his skin. And so, if and when the man was back to his normal self, he would bear the brunt of his anger, far worse than the beating he'd already received. He'd cop far worse than the pig. As he watched the man breathe, wrapped in his bandages, he gave thought to unplugging the machine or smothering him with a pillow or simply taking the body, throwing it over his shoulder, and tossing it into the water at Port Napier. But he wouldn't dare on account of his loyalty.

He passed by Sharon Wornkin's room on his way out and wanted to go in and apologise but instead he walked out of the hospital and drove his car down the main street to the pub.

Martin and Judah were seated at a table eating chicken parmigianas. There were more people here than on a usual Saturday afternoon, no doubt due to the festival. Dan behind the bar was keeping an eye on the lot of them.

'Your old man alright?' Martin asked when Brendan sat down.

'He will be, they reckon.'

'Good,' Martin said. He chewed. 'How hard is it to find one bloke?'

Judah swallowed and added, 'One old bloke.'

'Right. One old bloke.'

Brendan said, 'If we don't find him we're done here. In Newbury. You saw how Wornkin stood up to me. Without her under our thumb, we're done. She knows everything about how we do things.'

'If we make an example of this old bastard,' Martin said, 'Wornkin'll come back onside. Women like her always do. You watch.'

'Yeah.'

'I give us tonight. If we don't get him tonight, Wornkin'll keep pushing back. And you'll be done. Put Moore in the morgue by daylight and Wornkin will think twice before chucking you out. This town even have a morgue?'

Brendan said, 'It's in Trenton.'

flashing. Two officers standing there, probably more inside. An ambulance. Brendan accelerated.

'Slow down, idiot,' Judah said.

'What happened there, you think?' Sidney asked.

Brendan's eyes were twitchy and Sidney knew that whatever had transpired there had involved his brother. Probably the blood coating his shirt.

'You reckon that was the same cops parked outside Moore's?' Judah asked after they'd driven by.

'Probably,' Brendan said. 'Not many police to spare in Newbury. Or Trenton. Both small towns.'

'Good.'

'Hopefully that's where they'll be concentrated then, not on searching for Caleb.'

They drove on down the main street, past the pub. As they cleared Newbury and were passing the pastures on the road to Port Napier, Sidney ventured, 'What're you going to do with Martin?'

His body was now in the boot and Sidney imagined him trying to claw his way out.

Judah said. 'None of your bloody business.'

'Just asking,' Sidney said.

They drove past the service station, turned down to Port Napier. Sidney looked at the cemetery through the window and wondered if there should be streetlights down the rows of plots, so the dead might see where they were going as they walked around.

They turned left, went down a few streets, and at the end of one Brendan parked and turned off the lights.

'Good, no police car here,' Brendan said.

'Guess that was all of them back there then,' Judah said. 'You get out, see if Moore's come back. And be quick. They'll send somebody else out here soon to wait for Caleb to show up, I'm sure.'

'This is his house?' Sidney asked. The front garden was well kept.

'What do you think, dickhead?'

Brendan clambered from the car. There were no lights on in the house but at the front door an automatic light flicked on. Brendan stood stock-still, looking like the trespasser he was. When there was no movement from within, no door opening, no curtains parting, he kept moving. He knocked on the front door. Judah lit another cigarette and Sidney coughed. Brendan lifted the doormat, moved some rocks near the front step, could find no key. He turned to the car and shrugged in an exaggerated way. He walked back, opened the door, leaned his head in.

'They're not in,' he said.

'No shit,' Judah said.

'Well? Now what?'

'Go round the back.'

'Why?'

'Just see if you can get in that way. Make sure they're not in there.'

Brendan took a moment before shutting the door. Sidney watched him go around the corner of the house. The obnoxious cigarette smoke trickled up his nostrils. When Brendan reappeared he beckoned them to join him.

In the backyard, Brendan led them to an old shed. Beside it Sidney noticed freshly hewn dirt.

'There a torch?' Judah asked.

'Don't need a torch,' Brendan said.

'I can't see dick.'

Brendan sighed, then caught himself. 'I think there's one in the glove box.'

He went back to the car. Sidney risked a glance at this man who held them captive. He seemed monolithic in the moonlight and his cigarette made his face orange, some obscene traffic light. He turned to grin at Sidney, lifted his eyebrows.

'You see that light out there?' Judah said. He pointed out to sea.

Sidney saw a small light out in the darkness. Could be a fire. 'Someone's camping out on Snake Island,' he said.

'Snake Island?'

'It's just out there a bit. People camp there.'

Brendan returned with the torch and flicked it on, coating the shed they stood beside.

'This is what I wanted to show you,' he said. He shone the torch on an old engine, a tin of fuel, some battered life vests. 'Boat stuff,' he said. 'Reckon he's got a boat.'

'And yet the boat's not here,' Judah said, more to himself. He left the shed and looked again out over the water. 'Might be them out there.'

Brendan and Sidney joined him. 'Could be,' Brendan said.

'How long would it take to get over there?'

'Not sure,' Brendan said. 'An hour or two? Depends what kind of boat.'

'You got a boat?'

'Why would we have a boat?' Sidney said.

'Bloody hell,' Judah said. 'You always this whiny?' And then to Brendan, 'He always like this?'

When Brendan didn't reply, Judah said, 'We get a boat and head out there.'

'Might not be him, but,' Brendan said.

'Might not. You got any other ideas?'

'He could be anywhere by now,' Brendan said. 'He could've driven up to Melbourne.'

'In that car I slashed the tyres of, out in the bush?' Judah asked.

'His wife has a car, maybe.'

'Maybe,' Judah said. 'And maybe hers is that car parked right out front of the house.' He sucked on his cigarette. 'I want to get out there.'

'Probably a waste of time,' Sidney said.

'Quit bloody whining or I'll smack you.' Judah said this with little venom; just dissatisfaction.

Sidney stood silent, then said, 'That's two hours out and two hours back if it's not him.'

'What did I just say?' Judah lifted his hand as if to remove the cigarette from his mouth but instead clapped Sidney on the back of the head, hard. Sidney stumbled, and put up his own hands to steady himself, the movement jarring his already sore shoulder.

'Keep going,' Judah said, and raised his hand again.

Brendan said, 'He's right, though. That's a lot of wasted time if he's not out there.'

They studied the flickering light in the distance.

Brendan said, 'We could ask the neighbours.'

'Ask them what?'

'Whether he went out in his boat today.'

Judah took a moment and then nodded. 'Alright.' He stubbed his cigarette in the dirt and walked back down the driveway. Sidney followed him and Brendan to the house next door, a three-person army under cover of darkness.

~

They were soon motoring through the water. The darkness beneath them like blanketed sickness, souls gathered in evil perpetuity. The shotguns lay on the bottom of the boat, at Sidney's feet, clunking together. The old man's neighbours, after being threatened with violence by Judah, had been quick to give up what information they had. They'd seen Vernon head off that morning in his boat, his wife with him. He went out to Snake Island all the time, they said.

They hadn't put up a fight when the three of them took their boat. It had been a struggle to fit them all in, the two hulking giants and the diminutive Sidney. Judah sat in back with his feet up on the bench, Sidney squashed to the side near the just-in-case oars. The engine was garbage, barely strong enough to motor over this inky blackness. Any small swell would send them right back where they'd departed from.

Judah was grinning at him, like some horrible clown in the moonlight, his big teeth yellowed and his eyes wide. 'Bit of fun, hey?'

Up front, Brendan steered towards the flickering in the distance. As they grew closer they could make out the flames between the trees, and then two figures around the fire, their ghostly images hard to see for the warping heat and scrub.

Brendan said, 'Should we slow down?'

Judah nodded. 'Head around this other side where they won't hear us. Gun down the motor.'

Brendan did as he was told. They slowed to a crawl, barely any ripples floating by them. Sidney let his arm dangle over the side, almost willed a shark to take his fingers. Come on, you bastards. Swim to the surface and take my whole damn arm.

They drifted, Brendan steering. They waited until the couple left the fire. Must've gone inside their tent. Judah's feet were tapping. He lit a cigarette.

'Put that out,' Sidney said. He almost reached for it.

'Why?' Judah asked, mouth around the filter.

'They'll bloody see.'

Then he did reach for it. He swiped it from Judah's grinning mug and threw it in the water. Judah's grin fell, his chin followed, and he smacked his lips. 'You do that again, *you're* in the water.'

'Good.'

'With a hole in your chest.'

They decided to use the oars, Sidney and Brendan rowing, and soon passed by a smaller vessel, closer to the island. It looked as though nobody was in it and it was still some distance from shore. Drifting, though, untethered. A phantom boat.

Judah said, 'Put the boat in over there,' pointing at the shore.

'Should we check this floater out?' Brendan asked, nodding in its direction. 'Might be Moore's.'

'Who cares? We saw where they were. Don't need their boat.'

Sidney watched the boat as they glided by it. He saw what looked like a man's leg in there, up on the bench inside. The other two were keenly watching the shore now. Sidney decided not to mention it.

At the shoreline the water slapped against the hull. Brendan was first over the side, dragging the boat up onto the sand. Judah lumbered out with the shotguns and Sidney followed. Brendan made his way through the bush. The trees were huge and banded together like braided rope. The smell of salty mud. Sidney could feel it sticking to his shoes. He was sweating. The air was still.

Before him now this dreadful prospect. Judah had a shotgun and so did his brother a few paces ahead. They intended to shoot this old man who had sat beside him in the car as the kangaroo had struck him and, although it was not the old man's fault, he had still nursed him to the car, delivered him to his father. His father now mostly bandages in hospital.

He saw his daughter in all her smallness in her crib, just a newborn, suckling at a dummy, content in her beanie, her mittens, her socks. There with her kangaroo. His wife nearby asleep. What world was it they lived in where a man like Judah had the power to do whatever he pleased?

They came upon a clearing and in the midst of the cloying trees before them a ways away a smouldering fire, just embers burning under charcoal. They marched through the clearing like soldiers, carrying their weapons. Soon Judah motioned them to be still.

He whispered, 'Their tent's just through there.'

Sidney saw it then, billowing slightly in the breeze. An army-green colour.

'Now,' Judah whispered, 'we just walk right over this clearing and unload these into that tent there.' His eyebrows motioned towards the tent. 'Just destroy it. Then we take their bodies on that other boat and leave 'em somewhere in the centre of town. Nobody'll be messing with your family again.'

He held the shotgun like others might hold a loaf of bread. Like it was nothing. Sidney thought about his daughter. Thought about the type of man he was, the example he'd set her. How he'd live with himself after this, look her in the eye, try to teach her the world was good, that there *was* kindness, that there were people who'd care for her, love her truly. Knew that if he did this—if he helped pull the trigger—he'd never be able to show her the world he wanted her to know.

He yelled out Moore's name, almost unbidden. It seemed to come from his stomach, and then pulse through the trees. An animal roar. A warning for the old man. Brendan, upon hearing, must have seen the change in Judah's eye, the way his shoulders shifted, because he leapt onto the larger man and shouldered him to the ground. Judah grunted like a pig. Sidney tried to run but struggled in the mud. He had time to turn and look when he heard the shotgun, and saw his brother's wounded body fall from Judah and slap against the mud.

THIRTY-THREE

~

CALEB MOORE

The sound of voices woke him. He sat up quickly and saw how dark the night had become. The moon in the sky otherworldly. He saw another boat pulled into shore. Saw three figures huddled together, entering the overgrowth. The hint of whispers lost in the breeze. He also saw, with relief, how close he'd drifted to shore while he slept.

As his brain kicked back into gear and caught up with his situation he realised with deepening fear the three men were the Cahills of some description. Could pick out Brendan's silhouette easily, the lumbering monolith. Knew too his father and mother were probably asleep and had no idea what was going to happen. So he picked up his oar and started rowing. The boat spun, his arms still pained, the broken wrist just about useless. He abandoned it quickly and hopped out and found the water over his head height and so he swam with all he could, broken wrist and all, the cast waterlogged, up to the surface, gulping air. He kept swimming. Bloody arms need to work. The shore his lighthouse. It was slow going with the arm and he felt he would drown. He reached out with his legs and found soft ground beneath

278

them. He could walk, and did so. His body slowly emerged from the water and the cool breeze stuck the clothes to him. His arms in the fresh air, his hair cold. He was holding himself as he walked, trying to keep warm, and struggling. Soon he was entirely free of the ocean. He raced into the bush, over the gelatinous sand, trying to make his way to where his father used to camp on the other side of the island. He pried apart trees and soon found his fingers raw. Push on, push on. It was difficult going without a torch and he found his eyes were refusing to adjust.

You've done enough rotten things with your life, he told himself. Just do this one thing right. Just this one thing.

Soon he could make out his father's tent just through the trees. He almost yelled out but was silenced by the sound of voices nearby. He crouched down, stopped moving. There, almost upon him, were the three men.

The men were talking in low voices that didn't reach him. The largest of them was even bigger than Brendan and he had in hand a shotgun. Brendan too carried a gun. The smaller of the three was looking perplexed, and Caleb saw in his face the features of a Cahill.

This younger man turned away as the others readied themselves. Hard to tell what he was thinking but there was a surge to his chest, like he was holding his breath. Then he called out Vernon's name, a yell that sounded like it was borne from the earth itself. It shocked Caleb. The bigger man was immediately set upon by Brendan, as the younger one started to flee, and then the sound of a shotgun, cracking into the air, muffled by Brendan's body. He fell onto the earth and then scrambled away and into the bushes.

The other Cahill was now running but he hadn't made it halfway across the clearing before the man fired again. The shot struck him in the back of the head and he went down hard into the muck, like he'd been thrown there by a giant. His jagged arm was sticking up as if frozen, the mud around him sucking. The sound of the shot striking